SHADOW OF LOVE

Unable to control the exhilarating currents racing through her, Tracy threw caution to the wind. The passion Evan roused within her also alerted her as to how lonely she was. She realized how she'd starved herself from intimacy. "I love you, too," she heard herself say as she unbuttoned his shirt and eased it down over his broad shoulders. She slowly unsnapped his slacks and unzipped them, her fingers slightly grazing his masculinity. He let out a low growl and unzipped her dress. Without speaking, they made their way to his room, stopping to savor the sweetness of each other's lips and basking in adoration and affection. They did not stop to worry about the heap of clothing they left on the living room floor. They thought only of themselves and the ardent emotions that had been stirred up in both of them.

SHADOW OF LOVE

Marcella Sanders

ARABESQUE
BET BOOKS
BET Publications, LLC
www.bet.com
www.arabesquebooks.com

ARABESQUE BOOKS are published by

BET Publications, LLC
c/o BET BOOKS
One BET Plaza
1900 W Place NE
Washington, D.C. 20018-1211

All Kensington Titles, Imprints, and Distributed Lines are available at special quantity discounts for bulk purchases for sales promotions, premiums, fund-raising, and educational or institutional use. Special book excerpts or customized printings can also be created to fit specific needs. For details, write or phone the office of the Kensington special sales manager: Kensington Publishing Corp., 850 Third Avenue, New York, NY 10022, attn: Special Sales Department, Phone: 1-800-221-2647.

First Printing: March 2001

10 9 8 7 6 5 4 3 2 1
Printed in the United States of America

One

Tracy Wilson sauntered up the sidewalk, her yellow thong sandals fluttering lightly against the cracked cement. From the street she could still see the ocean, aquamarine waves swelling and rolling onto the white sand beach. She moved further up the walk, passing wooden beach homes and cherishing the triad winds lifting her hair. The sound of reggae music sifted through the air. Its timbre was as rich as the amber sun rays slipping into the horizon.

At that moment, she wondered why had she deprived herself of the well-deserved vacation, even if it was for only three days. St. Hope Isle was precisely what she craved to soothe her spirit. Tracy adjusted her shopping bag without slowing her gait as she approached a house. Fresh paint scented the air, blending with the fragrance of fresh fruit and a seafood smorgasbord arranged on a white-covered table. Adults and children mingled on the front lawn, dressed in an array of colors. Their attire appeared to contrast with their radiant personalities.

Tracy stopped at a table located at the edge of the yard, lingering over the lamps and white china trimmed in splintered gold designs. Placed against a brown bag in the center of the table was a sign written in grand red letters. BARGAINS. Tracy took off her sunglasses and dropped them inside her shopping bag.

"Can I help you?" A tall woman with skin the color of brown toast called to her.

"Yes," Tracy answered, observing how the breeze blew the woman's long, green dress up around her ankles.

"Is there anything in particular that you want to buy?" the woman asked, arranging a cup that had slid from its rightful place.

"I'm not sure," Tracy said, noticing the woman pull her green scrap over the silver strands of hair that peeked from underneath. "I am interested in the bag." She moved closer to the table. "Other than that, I don't know if there's anything here that I need."

"If you don't buy, you'll miss a bargain." The woman's crimson-red lips spread into a smile.

"What's in the bag?"

The woman answered Tracy between soft, rich laughter. "To tell you the truth, it's junk." She moved the sign, laying it on top of the chipped china, and held the bag out to Tracy.

Tracy set her shopping bag down, took the bag from the woman and looked inside. "It doesn't look like junk to me," she said, removing a faux ruby necklace and a pair of matching earrings. She held the jewelry up for better inspection, like an expert examining jewelry. The imitation necklace and earrings sparkled against the setting sun.

"Trust me. It's junk." The woman's laughter was now richer than her previous chuckles.

Tracy reached inside the bag again, selecting a rather long, black, wrinkled leather case. With the tip of her thumb, she flipped the top, revealing faded scarlet velvet. "How much do you want for the jewelry?" Tracy asked, realizing that the women participating in the Women in Need of Help program could benefit from the jewelry. The fake trinkets would be perfect, accessorizing the secondhand suits donated to the program that provided women with business attire.

"I'll take twenty dollars," the woman said, extending her hand before Tracy could take her purse from her shopping bag.

"What do you think this is, some fancy department store?" Tracy asked, determined to pay less than the asking price.

"No, but why would you buy this stuff anyway?" The woman seemed to study Tracy. "You don't look like a woman who wears fake jewelry."

Placing one hand on her hip, Tracy held the jewelry bag with her free hand. "I plan to donate the jewelry to a women's program."

"Okay. Give me fifteen dollars."

"Ten." Tracy was firm with her decision. Besides, her older sister, Hannah, had trained her to shop well. Tracy decided that if the woman continued to challenge her, she might walk away from the table paying less than the ten dollars she offered.

"All right . . . ten dollars," the woman said. "And I'll just throw in some herbal tea leaves for an extra two bucks." She held up a clear plastic bag filled with infinitesimal green leaves and dangled them in front of Tracy.

"I don't know," Tracy answered, squinting to get a better look at the small leaves. "What are they good for?"

"Aha, you're interested."

"I'm curious," Tracy replied, wondering if the herbs held some magic potion to cure her hay fever.

"These leaves are for your man." The woman swallowed as if mentioning the herbs conjured their delightful flavor.

Tracy noticed the woman watching her, as if looking for scattered signs of admission that she needed to attract a man with magical herbs.

"No, I think I'll pass," Tracy said. Drake Wilson had been dead for more than two years, and during the few years of their marriage, she didn't need herbs, weeds, or twigs to inflame his passion for her.

"Fine," the woman said, "but some women are not so lucky."

"I wouldn't know. But even if I bought the herbs, the price for the entire sale would be less than twelve dollars." Tracy used the haggling technique she'd learned from Hannah.

"All right. You're cheap," the woman said, reaching inside the box for another plastic bag. "These herbs are for your man too, but. . . ." She pointed a long, red fingernail at Tracy.

"I told you. I'm not interested in buying your herbs." Tracy reached inside her shopping bag to take out her purse, preparing to pay for the jewelry and walk to her hotel. "I don't have a man," Tracy said. Her husband, Drake, died in a plane crash and she hadn't had a man in her life since.

"What?" the woman asked, a shocked expression shadowing her face. "A fine-looking young woman like yourself, and you don't have a man in your life? Long black hair," she complimented, "nice smile, long legs, and cheeks that look as if they'd bleed if I pinched them. Or is that blush?"

Tracy disregarded the woman's compliments and offered her a crisp twenty-dollar bill.

"I could've sold these herbs to any woman on this island for twenty dollars." She took the money and fished around in her dress pocket for change. "Are you from the States?" She held the change out to Tracy.

Tracy nodded, taking the money.

"What city are you from, New York?"

"No, I'm from Atlanta."

"Georgia. I went there once." She held up the herbs. "Are you sure you don't want these herbs?"

"I don't have any use for the herbs." Tracy looked over her shoulder, after sensing that someone was standing behind her. She turned to get a better look at him. He was a muscular man with light skin and he appeared to be about six feet tall.

"They're good for colds, flu, and hay fever," the woman said.

For a minute, Tracy contemplated her offer. Hannah had continued their mother's old-folk remedies after their mother had died. Hannah purchased teas from the health food store. When she didn't have enough money, she went to their elderly neighbor and returned with a liquid concoction for Tracy's flu and hay fever symptoms. "I'll give you a dollar for the herbs."

"This bag is worth . . ."

"One dollar," Tracy said, turning again, annoyed that the tall, light-skinned gentleman was standing right behind her. She moved to the end of the table to get a better look at him. His eyes were like black coal, and his mouth was wide and unsmiling. His body was built like a professional wrestler.

"*Shew!*" The woman blew a whistle between her teeth, passing the herbs to Tracy and taking the dollar. "Cheap."

"Have a good evening," Tracy said, moving down the street and away from the woman's audible grumble.

Satisfied with her purchases from the island store and the jewelry she'd bought from the yard sale, Tracy walked to her hotel, enjoying the array of kaleidoscopic flowers decorating the grounds and scenting the air with a sweet aroma.

This is heaven, Tracy mused. Then the sound of impatient footsteps cut into her pondering. She glanced over her shoulder and recognized the tall man she'd seen earlier. She wasn't certain if he was following her, but she quickened her pace. His footsteps matched hers, pounding swiftly against the concrete.

Fear coiled inside Tracy and rose to her throat, and she thought that she would suffocate. She hurried, passing shops that were closing for the evening.

Rushing around the corner, half running, she submerged herself in the crowd, which formed a line waiting to enter one of the island's favorite restaurants.

She could smell spicy crab meat and garlic shrimp. The sound of reggae music and bongo drums filtered out from the restaurant. Tracy moved far enough out of the crowd to see if the man was still following her. She saw him standing at the edge of the curb, looking left and then right, and then he turned back toward the house. Feeling that she was safe, she hailed a cab to her hotel.

Once inside her hotel room, Tracy packed and prepared to take the next flight home. Her purpose for taking a weekend vacation was to relax and to get away from the uproar in Atlanta and her job at Maxwell Realty. If she had wanted to be chased, she could've stayed in Atlanta and feared being followed and robbed by the thief that was threatening the city.

Then there was her sister, Hannah, who insisted that Tracy relieve her one night a week at Hannah and her husband Jordan's dinner club, so that Hannah could attend college night classes.

Tracy sat at the desk in her hotel room and called her best friend, Regina Telfair. After several rings, Regina answered.

"Tracy, I thought you would've found a party to go to by now!" Regina sounded disappointed that Tracy was calling instead of having fun.

"Regina, I'm leaving the island."

"What happened to all the fun you planned to have?"

"Girl, I went shopping, and on my way to the hotel, I believe a man was chasing me."

"You should've stopped and let him catch you." Regina's voice was filled with mischief.

Tracy joined her laughter. After Drake's death, Regina joined Hannah, taking the opportunity to play matchmaker. She arranged dinners, parties, and blind dates for her. *It is a shame that none of the dates worked out,* Tracy pondered. She simply did not like the men. Besides, she and Drake had been soul mates, and no other man could compare.

"Tracy, are you telling me that you went all the way to St. Hope Isle and aren't having just a tiny bit of fun?"

Initially, Tracy *had* planned to have fun. However she hadn't gone to meet a prospective lover—as Regina was implying. She had enough work in her life to keep her occupied, and she didn't need a romantic relationship. "Well, maybe I'll go to the hotel party tonight."

"I'm glad you called me. You need to enjoy yourself before returning to the rat race," Regina said, then added, "You have fun."

"Sure. We'll talk next week," Tracy said, hanging up.

Unable to relax, Tracy checked her messages. A new agent from Maxwell Realty was interested in renting one of her apartments to an underprivileged tenant.

Drake's parents had left four apartment buildings to him after they died. Now that he was gone, the buildings belonged to her. She hadn't changed the way things were operated. The manager had taken care of the building for years, and Tracy let him remain in that position.

Acting braver than she felt, Tracy decided not to waste her time worrying when she could be having fun. She'd promised Regina that she was going to the party. Why waste a weekend fearing a man who was probably not chasing her in the first place?

She took a shower and dressed in a black, two-piece bathing suit, a long, black wrap skirt, and a pair of gold sandals. She applied just a touch of apple-red lipstick to compliment her peachy complexion. Tracy brushed her hair until it bounced with body, then headed downstairs to the hotel patio.

Multicolored lights lit the patio, giving the pool water a polychromatic effect. Music floated out, echoing against the night, while hotel residents danced, moving rhythmically to the beat of the tropical sounds that blended with their laughter and conversation.

"May I have this dance?"

Tracy turned her attention to an island-accented voice behind her. Her mouth opened, but she was unable to speak. She backed away from the tall, light-skinned man that she believed had followed her earlier.

"I-I don't want to dance," she finally spoke.

"I saw you at my old friend's house," he said, flashing a smile.

To Tracy, his smile didn't reach his cold black

eyes. She was taught that eyes were the windows to one's soul. *If this is the case, this man doesn't seem to have a soul,* she thought.

"I'm Frank Johnson," he said, extending his broad hand.

Tracy allowed him to give her hand a flimsy shake. "Tracy Wilson," she replied.

"How long do you plan to stay on the island Tracy?" Frank asked.

"Not long." She deliberately didn't tell him of her plans to leave. There was something about him that she didn't trust. She lifted her chin, looking into his frosty, black eyes.

"Were you following me today?" She asked, trying to read his facial expression, his eyes, and his body movement. But nothing registered.

"Why would I do a thing like that—chase a pretty lady like yourself? Are you crazy?" He smiled, showing broad, white teeth. "Let's dance."

Against her better judgment, she danced with him, and to her surprise, she began to enjoy herself. When the music changed to a slower beat, Frank reached out for her.

"I think I'll sit this one out," Tracy said, going to a patio table. A waiter walked over carrying a tray filled with drinks. He set a frosty, purple concoction in front of her. She gave him a friendly smile and sipped the fruity, icy liquid.

"Where do you live, Tracy?" Frank pulled out a chair and sat across from her.

The uneasy feeling returned. She didn't feel comfortable telling him where she was from. His question rang like a silent alarm, warning her to withhold personal information and keep a safe distance between them. "Why do you want to know?" she asked, taking another sip of the drink.

"I might want to visit you."

"Excuse me," she said, getting up from the table.

"I didn't mean to upset you," Frank said. "Maybe we could get together and go out on a date."

"I don't date." Tracy said. "Good night."

Tracy walked to her room. She had a couple of hours before her flight back to the States. She called for wake-up service from the hotel management, then went to bed. She drifted in and out of sleep, until she finally sank into a deep slumber and began to dream.

Drake's voice was edged with fright. His milk-chocolate complexion seemed to have darkened with fear for her. "Run, Tracy." He stood at the edge of the ocean, his long arms motioning backward as if he wanted her to cross the water. In her confused, dreaming state, she thought he wanted her to come to him. When she headed in his direction, he backed away, pointing across the ocean.

"Where . . . where do you want me to go?" she cried. The ringing phone drew her out of a fitful sleep.

Tracy had dreamed about Drake many times. And her dreams were all pleasant. But this time he frightened her.

For a few minutes, she lay contemplating the dream and the days she'd spent on the island.

The only fun she'd had was shopping. Maybe she'd chosen the wrong island. Her broker, Keith Maxwell, mentioned that he'd practically grown up on the island. He promised her that she would have fun.

Tracy showered, dressed, and took a cab to the airport.

Frank Johnson dialed the number to the computer store on the other side of the island. "St. Hope Isle's finest," he mumbled under his breath, which reeked of whiskey. "Let's see how fine you really are, old buddy."

He leaned back and waited for the party to answer.

"I need to see you this morning, at the pier." He slammed the phone back on the receiver and wheeled around, staring out the window. *It isn't fair that I have suffered while my so-called best friend walked away free,* Frank fumed. *When I'm finished with him, he's going to wish he'd spent fifteen years behind bars too.* A hollow laugh rose from the pit of Frank Johnson's stomach, gravitated to his throat, and slipped past his lips, echoing against the unpainted walls that divided the two rooms in his dilapidated shack.

Two

Evan stood on the pier. It was the same pier where Frank had tried to escape the authorities fifteen years ago. He looked out across the ocean. Speed boats raced across the water, no doubt to one of the luxurious homes on the opposite side of the beach, while sea gulls dove into the waves, fishing for their lunch.

Evan's life was in order—or that's what he'd thought until he received the call from Frank Johnson. He pulled his blue fishing hat further down onto his head. He didn't have the slightest idea what Frank wanted from him now.

Many years ago, when he was a teen, he and Frank were friends. Frank and his uncles were modern-day pirates, hijacking boats and yachts, robbing the owners of their vessels and all the goods. When Evan became friends with Frank against his father's will, he joined them on their trips, traveling the high seas in the blackness of the night.

While Evan's father made voyages importing cargo and goods, Evan sat quietly in the back of Frank's family boat as the men seized helpless victims.

Evan watched intensely, not getting involved, since he was traveling with the men for two reasons. His first reason was as an act of rebellion against his father, who forced him to live on the island, away from his mother in Atlanta. His second reason was to make his stepmother worry, hoping she would talk his father into sending him back to Atlanta.

Evan never robbed any of the vessels. However, he was almost seriously injured the last time he went out with Frank and his uncles. One of Frank's uncles cruised up to a boat, pretending to need assistance. The crew obviously realized that the men intended to rob them. A fight broke out, and guns were fired. One of the uncles tossed Evan a pistol, ordering him to shoot. He aimed the pistol and fired, missing his target on purpose when he realized that the man worked for his father. To add insult to injury, the boat that Frank's uncles were attempting to rob belonged to Evan's father.

Nonetheless, Evan was called "The Black Pirate." How he managed to stay clear of trouble was only grace from a higher force than himself, he finally concluded after growing older.

His only misfortune was being hit in his eye. While the victims fought for their lives, their vessel, and the goods aboard, Evan was struck. When he returned to a conscious state, he was aboard a boat belonging to his father.

Evan ran a long, square finger over his neatly shaven beard. He'd learned later from his father that Frank jumped overboard and was unsuccessful in his attempt to escape the Bahamian shores. He was captured by the authorities and sent to prison for fifteen years.

The roar from a boat's motor jerked Evan back to the present. He watched Frank's muscular frame climb from the rusty vessel and make its way up on the deck. Frank's skin seemed lighter than Evan remembered. He looked older and gaunt, as if the time he served in prison had been his worst enemy. Evan looked toward the heavens, thanking his father for saving his life. "What do you want, Frank?"

"Is that all you can say?" Frank grinned, baring his teeth.

"We don't have much to talk about." Evan straightened and faced Frank. "How have you been?"

Frank moved over and stood beside Evan. "I thought I was going to be fine, until I went to your daddy's old house." He folded his arms across his chest. "You remember the night I went to jail . . . don't you?"

"We were kids," Evan said, realizing the grudge that Frank obviously held.

"No, you were a kid. I was a man," he said, tapping his hand against his broad chest. "You were on the boat for the ride and to make your daddy worry. I was on the boat to help feed myself and my sister."

"Are you blaming me?"

"Of course I am. Your daddy made sure you were off this island and in another country before sunset the next day."

"I'm not going to stand around and discuss what happened years ago," Evan said. He had meetings to attend and phone calls to make. "Frank, if you choose to live in the past, it's fine with me, but I've moved on."

"I *am* in the past, Evan. My future ended on this pier years ago." Frank moved closer to Evan. "What do you want from me?" Evan whispered.

"I want you to do something for me," Frank said, reaching in his shirt pocket and taking out a small, black note pad. "I need you to do me a favor." He gave Evan the pad.

Evan took one glance at the information on the paper. "The woman's name was Tracy Wilson. She worked for Maxwell Realty. I can't do this."

"Oh, but you *will* do it, Evan." Frank grinned. "You see, I know a few guys who're interested in computers." His grin turned into an ugly smirk. "Your store seems to have the stuff they're shopping for."

Anger scratched at Evan's insides as his past reared its ugly head, promising to destroy his life after all. He couldn't allow that to happen. He had worked hard at every area of his life. He and his brother, Keith, were finally close again. His father was deceased, but his stepmother had forgiven him and his mother still loved him. His aunt no longer reminded him that he was the Maxwell family's worst nightmare. He and his partner, Grant LaCount, owned several respected computer businesses. Their newest store was opening in Atlanta in a few weeks, and Frank was standing in front of him asking him to steal. "Have you lost your mind?"

"No. But if you don't take care of this, I'm afraid you'll lose your businesses," Frank threatened.

"I'm not worried about you destroying anything I own," Evan stated firmly. It seemed that prison had made Frank meaner than Evan remembered. He glanced down at the pad again. "How did you get this information?"

"The Internet, man." Frank folded his arms across his chest.

"If my equipment is destroyed or stolen, you'll deal with me first and the authorities later," Evan promised.

"Evan, you have to do this for me."

"I don't *have* to do anything."

"I can't get a job, and without money, I might as well have stayed in prison."

"I don't remember you owning any valuables," Evan said to Frank, remembering that Frank was the most destitute person he'd known on the island.

"It belonged to my grandmother. To keep my uncles from stealing it, I hid it in your daddy's house." Frank replied.

Evan frowned. "Okay, I'll see what I can do."

"Now you're talking with sense." Frank chuckled.

"On one condition," Evan said. "I'm not forcing the person to *give* me anything."

"Good. It doesn't matter how you do it, as long as it's done."

Evan watched Frank turn and head back to

his boat. He was certain that Frank meant every word when he threatened to steal from him, even if it was after he'd taken care of the "favor."

Evan walked to his office, passing dock workers assembled at a table in front of a small eatery, lunching on cod and cold soft drinks. The cod scented the warm air, reminding him how much he hated the food. He had eaten fish on the nights that he'd spent on the boat with Frank and his uncles, because it was all they'd taken with them.

He suspected that his best friend, Grant, would think he was suffering from temporary insanity once he told him his plan to help Frank. But, he'd rather have Grant thinking he'd lost his mind than have Frank out of work and stealing from them.

When he finally reached his office, he went straight to Grant. Evan found him doling out orders in the shipping department.

"I need to talk to you," Evan said, eyeing his friend closely.

"What's going on, Maxwell?" Grant asked, moving away from the boxes. He ducked his head out of the way of a box jutting from a top shelf and moved down the aisle, tailing Evan. His light brown eyes seemed to hold a look of concern.

"I met with Frank Johnson today," Evan said once they were in the corridor, walking to Evan's office.

"When did he get out of prison?"

"I didn't ask, but I'm sure he hasn't been a free man for a very long time."

Evan opened the office door and walked into a cool, spacious room. He sat in a chair across from his desk, while Grant sank down on the tan leather sofa.

"What did he want?" Grant asked, his concern deepening.

Evan handed Grant the pad with the information Frank had given to him. "Rehabilitation didn't work for him," Grant said, returning the pad to Evan and getting up to sit on the edge of the desk. "Evan, he hates you."

"I know that," Evan said. "But I'll do just about anything to keep his sticky hands out of our business."

"This guy is crazy," Grant said. "We can call the police and put him back behind bars."

"Right, and while he's behind bars, our business will be vandalized by thugs he hired to do his filthy work."

"Are you actually going through with this?"

"I have no intentions of doing anything to wreck my life." Evan frowned, removing his hat to unmask thick, black, wavy hair. "However, I intend to take care of this matter."

"Be careful."

Evan shrugged his wide shoulders. "I'll be fine." He got up and went to the telephone, making a reservation for the next flight to Atlanta.

Three

Only four tables awaited guests with reservations at Hannah's dinner club before the employee Tracy was filling in for finally arrived.

"Did you get your car repaired?" Tracy asked the young man, who looked frustrated and exhausted.

"No, and I almost missed the bus," he said, preparing to work.

Tracy just smiled. She could imagine how he felt. She smoothed her hands over her short, black dress and walked behind the bar to see if Betty had arrived. She found Jordan, her brother-in-law, behind the bar, serving rum and Coke to a customer.

"Tracy, Betty will be in shortly." Jordan flashed a grin at her. "I have to talk to Hannah before she leaves for school. Will you take over here?"

"Sure," Tracy said, noticing that his toffee skin seemed to glow with appreciation. Tracy thought that Hannah and Jordan had a special love. Jordan was quiet and seemed to do whatever he could to make Hannah happy. He wasn't the tall, muscular man that most women dreamed of. He was of medium height, with a nice smile, and with just enough gray edging his temples.

"Thanks, Tracy," Jordan said, hurrying to catch Hannah.

Tracy went to the cabinet where she kept her low-heeled shoes. She slipped out of her three-inch heels, exchanging them for the comfortable flats, and washed her hands.

"Can I help you?" Tracy asked the man who slid on a stool just as she returned.

"I'll have an iced tea," he replied.

Tracy filled his order, hoping that he didn't have a sad story to tell. After her island excursion, she was not in the mood. If Hannah wasn't her sister, she wouldn't dream of tending the bar or greeting customers. She had slept the entire day before, after she arrived in town and almost refused Hannah when she asked Tracy to fill in for Betty and the new employee.

"Ooh-wee! Woman, what did you put in this tea, grain alcohol?"

Tracy studied him carefully before answering. His tan suit looked tailored. His salt-and-pepper hair gave him a distinguished look. "I'm sorry, I thought you wanted iced tea with alcohol." She reached for his drink.

He wrapped his fingers around the glass. "I wanted regular iced tea, the kind my wife prefers that I drink," he replied chuckling.

"I misunderstood." She reached for the drink again.

"Oh no, I'll drink it. She's not here." He took a swig from the glass, then turned to the woman beside him and started to tell her about the events of his day.

A smile settled on Tracy's lips. By now, she should've known the routine. From time to time, a few men and women often settled at the bar without their spouses and spent the evening flirting with any available man or woman that sat next to them.

"Goodness, this place is busy tonight!" Betty had arrived and stood beside Tracy. "How are you, Miss Tracy?"

"I'm okay," Tracy said, recalling how her short vacation had been spoiled. However, Betty looked as fresh and crisp as ever. Her long, black hair fell over her coffee-colored shoulders, and her makeup was applied to perfection. Betty could have easily passed for a thirty-five-year-old, instead of her forty years.

"You're telling me that after you went to St. Hope Isle, you're just *okay?*"

"Yes," Tracy answered, not going into details with Betty about her frightening experience on the island.

"Child, I vacationed in St. Hope Isle once, and I never saw so many handsome men in my life."

"Betty, I didn't go to the island looking for a man." Tracy scanned the crowded dining room. Beautiful couples sat in the dimly lit room, dining and drinking wine, while engaging in quiet conversations fused with silky, romantic music.

"I know. You went to the island to relax. You could've relaxed at home."

Tracy didn't respond to Betty's comment. Instead, she focused on the happy couples in the dining room, realizing that a life filled with love and romance was over for her. She took a cloth and wiped the space on the bar where a gentleman had just left.

"I'll have a Scotch on the rocks."

Tracy glanced up at the sound of the island accent and looked into charcoal gray eyes. "Sure, Keith," she said, wondering what had made her broker come to Hannah's for a drink. She had never seen him in Hannah's before, neither had she seen him casually dressed. His blue sports shirt made him appear more relaxed. Tracy dismissed this, realizing that people were full of surprises. She poured the drink and set it in front of him, planning to go home, as soon as she served the drink.

"I'm Evan . . . Evan Maxwell," the gentleman corrected her.

Tracy was too stunned to reply; she could only stare. He was the very image of Keith Maxwell. The same cappuccino complexion, identical charcoal-gray eyes, and his close-shaved beard was also the same as Keith's. Even Evan's wide palms, and square fingers and nails were a perfect match—except for the missing wedding band. She checked his ring finger to see if it had a lighter shade circling his finger.

"I'm Keith's twin," Evan asserted, dispensing a quick chuckle to put an end to her confusion.

"It's good to meet you." She smiled at him. "I'm Tracy Wilson."

Evan reached across the bar's counter, extending his hand. "Tracy Wilson," he repeated her name, then released her and settled back, taking a sip from his Scotch.

"You're visiting your brother?" Tracy asked, dismissing the strange sensation that passed through her from the touch of Evan's hand.

"Yes. I'm also here on business." Evan smiled at her. "And I need to talk to you."

Tracy couldn't imagine what Evan Maxwell wanted to talk to her about. If he wanted to buy a house or condo, he could always go to his brother. "Sorry, I'm leaving in a few minutes," Tracy replied. She never understood why some people felt free to discuss their problems with a stranger. Since she wasn't a therapist, she chose not to listen.

"Maybe we can talk another time," he said, not giving up on his request to talk to her.

"I'm sorry, but I really have to go," Tracy said, annoyed at his persistence.

"Tomorrow night?" he probed relentlessly.

"Can you give me a hint as to what you'd like to discuss?" Tracy asked, noticing that his penetrating gaze seemed to hold a special message for her.

"Why don't we discuss it over dinner Friday night?" He reached out and touched her hand.

"I don't know, I'll have to check my appointment book," Tracy said, trying to remember if she had a house to show on the evening in question. She struggled with the annoying sensation that raced through her from Evan's second touch.

"If you'll give me your number, I'll call you and we can set up a date," he said.

Tracy didn't respond right away. Instead, she went to get her purse and shoes. On her way back to him, she took a business card from her purse and gave it to him.

While taking the card, he covered her hand with his.

"Thanks," Evan said.

Tracy met his gaze again, agitating the slow-lingering, irritating sensation circulating through her and settling near her heart. She quickly tried to dismiss the unsettling sensation, which refused her diminishing command.

"I would like to call you at home," Evan said, after looking at the phone, pager, and voicemail numbers on the card.

Tracy didn't give her home number to clients and strangers. Although he was Keith's brother, she didn't know him. "You can beep me," she said, turning away from him.

"Good night, Betty," she said, and headed out back to her car, stopping to ask one of the men working in the kitchen to walk with her to the parking lot. A thief was on the loose, terrorizing the city. The authorities warned men and women to be careful, because the thief was considered armed and dangerous.

Just as she stopped near a young man who was slicing a thick, round carrot, she saw Jordan walking through the back door. Instead of wearing his usual khaki pants, matching khaki shirt, and thick-soled black shoes, he was dressed in a pair of a black trousers and a beige silk shirt.

"Well, aren't we dressed up tonight," Tracy said, going over to him and asking her brother-in-law to walk with her instead.

"I had a meeting," Jordan stated, following her out to her car.

"Some meeting."

"Are you suggesting that I didn't have a meeting?"

"No," Tracy said. Lately, she had begun to wonder about Jordan's meetings. But she kept these concerns to herself. He'd been nothing but loving to her sister. It was about time he dressed up. Tracy was almost certain that dressing nicely made him feel better. She thanked Jordan for walking with her to her car.

All that Tracy could think about while driving home was her conversation with Evan and his reasons for wanting to talk to her. No doubt Evan was like most men that had their evening drinks at Hannah's bar while waiting for a table. They wanted to vent about their jobs or personal problems. But Evan was different. Or was he? She allowed the question to trek across her mind as she remembered the feel of his touch, and the sensation that danced from deep within her.

Tracy drove off the main highway into her neighborhood, passing two-story houses that rested on thick lawns, surrounded by tall pines and beds of multicolored flowers. As she drove, she doubted seriously that Evan would remember to call her.

She eased into her driveway, took the garage remote from the car's compartment, and raised the garage door. She drove inside, parking next to Drake's red truck, which she still hadn't gotten around to selling. Each time she said she would stop at the store and buy a sale sign, she'd always broken her promise with the same excuse, telling herself that she had other important things to take care of. She realized deep within her soul that she was hanging on to a part of her husband. She also understood that she had to let go, but it was hard.

She got out of the car, unlocked her kitchen door, and went inside. She flipped the light switch, filling her kitchen with an amber glow, and went to the foyer, picking up the mail from the floor. As she looked at the envelopes, she realized that she was holding an advertisement addressed to Drake.

It was moments like these that made tears catch in her throat and her memories scroll back to the past, like silent pictures from an old View-Master. Instead of going up to her bedroom, she sat on the sofa in her living room, holding the ad and staring at her and Drake's wedding pictures on the mantel.

They were a happy couple, with life promising them only the best it had to offer. They had each other and their real-estate careers, and as a wedding gift to themselves, they'd purchased their dream home.

She looked around the room at the furniture she and Drake had chosen. The beige living room set, glass tables, tall, green silk plants protruding from silver pots, and vertical blinds covering the wide front window that resembled gold ribbons. These were the choices they'd made together. A cloud with two soaring robins painted on canvas hanging behind the sofa was Drake's symbol of them accomplishing their hopes and dreams. To Tracy, the painting was an indication of how free she and Drake's life had been, with not a care in the world. They only needed their love to survive, grow, and win.

If only I had been patient, she reflected, placing the envelope on the coffee table and recalling that tragic night. She had finally closed her first big sale on one of the most luxurious homes in the city. Instead of waiting until Drake returned from his business trip to tell him the exciting news, she called him and insisted that he come home as soon as possible. Drake agreed to take an earlier flight, in order to be home in time for her celebration. His flight crashed, and her world collapsed. It was her fault. She didn't care how many times Hannah, Regina, and Betty told her that she was not to blame.

Tracy got up and went to her room. It seemed that she had lost the people she loved most. Her father left home, leaving her mother to raise her and Hannah alone. When she was eleven, her mother died, and Hannah raised her. Now that Drake was dead, she made up her mind that she would never involve herself in an intimate relationship again.

As she lay between cool, crisp, lavender sheets, her thoughts wandered to Evan Maxwell. What did he want to talk to her about?

* * *

Evan completed the interview with the young woman. Finding an assistant who could manage the business while he and Grant weren't around was beginning to present a problem.

The woman that left his office minutes ago was far from the assistant he had in mind. First of all, her attire was too alluring, and she wore too much makeup. Her black hair was pinned into an up-do style. He didn't understand if she'd just left a night club and then came in for the interview, or if it was her regular hairstyle.

He leaned back, resting his head against the high-back leather chair, waiting for his next appointment before he went to lunch with Keith.

"Come in," he said to the knock on his office door.

An older woman dressed in a blue suit and white blouse, wearing blue pumps and a serious face, walked into his office. Her hair was styled into a classic coiffure, and her makeup was applied as if professionally done.

"I'm Dolores Williams," she said, sitting down before Evan could offer her a chair.

Evan knew that she was the assistant he would be hiring before he even interviewed her. He checked her application and asked several questions, learning that she had a degree in business administration. The last company she worked for had moved to another country.

"I will be in and out of the office for a few weeks," Evan informed her, telling her that he was returning to the island. "I expect you to handle things here." It was then that he noticed she was smiling for the first time.

"When would like for me to start?" Dolores asked.

"The beginning of next week will be fine." Evan said, extending his hand. "Welcome to Maxwell and LaCount Computers."

After Dolores left, Evan looked at the business card Tracy had given him the night he was at Hannah's dinner club. She was a real estate agent at Keith's office. As he looked at her name on the card, he remembered that the name was the same one Frank wrote on the paper he gave to him the day they met on the pier.

The last time Evan visited Keith at his office, older male and female agents worked in his office. He didn't know his brother's employees were now young and attractive. Tracy was tall, with a nice shape. Her lips were full and inviting, and her complexion was clear and smooth, complementing her long black wavy hair.

The "favor" he was doing for Frank posed a few complications now. His plan was to ask for what he wanted, and hopefully the woman would give it to him. Things had changed. He hadn't expected to find Tracy Wilson working in Hannah's. It just happened that he was looking for a place to have dinner and a drink. The tour map suggested several restaurants, and Hannah's was on the list. The ad said that Hannah's menu was old-fashioned, down-home cooking. But he never got a chance to eat, since he didn't have a reservation. He had a drink and settled on fast food later that evening.

To his surprise, he'd found Tracy. She was tall with curves in all the right places; with wide, full lips with just a hint of lipstick and inches and inches of long, black, thick hair. Her skin was smooth and rosy like a Georgia peach. All he wanted was to ask Tracy for a date.

Evan dismissed these thoughts, considering that Tracy Wilson was probably head-over-heels in love with some Southern gentleman.

Evan headed out to meet Keith for lunch. For a brief moment, he hoped that he'd see Tracy while at Maxwell Realty. If he were lucky, she might join *him* for lunch, instead of Keith. *I can drop by Keith's house before I leave for the island, and have dinner with him and his family anytime,* he mused, with visions of Tracy clicking through his mind.

Tracy walked into the cool lobby off Peachtree Street, out of the blistering noon day sun. She took a tissue from her purse and wiped away the perspiration beading at her temples and forehead before taking the elevator to her office.

The pale-pink, sleeveless dress that she wore could have been an overcoat for all the coolness that it provided. She noticed that the tellers in the bank across the lobby from the elevator were perched behind their stations, which reminded her to cash her Travelers Cheques from her trip to St. Hope Isle.

The elevator's door slid open and she stepped inside, enjoying the soft music filling the wide steel space and the crisp air flowing from the air vents. She kept her mind free from recalling her surprise meeting with Evan Maxwell and instead focused on her pending appointment.

Tracy stepped off the elevator and walked a few doors down to Maxwell Realty's waiting area. Prospective buyers and renters were seated anxiously on the edges of the green leather sofa and chairs.

Tracy spoke to the potential clients and regular customers as she eased past the coffee table, to the tea and ice dispensers near the back of the room. Tracy stopped at the ice machine and pressed the button allowing the machine to dole out several pieces of ice in the tall cup before she filled it with dark, sweet, old-fashioned tea.

Upon entering the office she shared with Regina, Tracy opened the blinds, allowing bands of sunlight to brighten the room. She sat at her desk, taking the folder for her next appointment from the tray and placing it in front of her. She ripped the edge off a sugar pack and sprinkled the white crystals into her tea. Stirring slowly, she allowed visions of Evan Maxwell's handsome face to sashay through her mind.

Sipping the iced tea, Tracy forced the visions of Evan out of her head and opened the file to study it. No matter how hard she tried, she couldn't stop thinking about Evan. She set the tea down and continued to go over the property comparable sheet, listing the prices of the homes last sold in her potential sellers' neighborhoods.

Again, her mind wandered back to Evan. *Why*

haven't I met him before, she wondered, looking out her window and surveying the towering buildings extending toward the sky.

Tracy lifted the cup and traced the rim with her finger. Keith had never mentioned that he had a brother. But then again, Keith never mentioned much of anything if it wasn't in reference to real estate.

Tracy had just turned her attention back to the folder when Regina walked in. Regina's new haircut was layered and feathered on top. The sides and back were shaved close to her head.

"Like it?" Regina smiled, swirling herself around so that Tracy could get a better view of the short, sassy hair style.

"I love it," Tracy said as Regina set her attaché case on her desk. "I'm thinking of a similar style for myself," Tracy added, seriously thinking about keeping her promise to cut her hair if the weather didn't cool soon.

"I finally closed on that warehouse," Regina said, sitting at her desk, a fresh smile lighting up her face.

"Congratulations. I didn't close my deal this morning," she said, a twinge of disappointment whetting her voice.

"Did the buyer change his mind?"

"No, he didn't have enough money for the closing." Tracy tapped her finger against the desktop, stressing her disappointment. "I wish he had informed me of his finances days ago." Again she turned her attention back to the folder.

"How did you enjoy your trip?" Regina asked.

"I have had better vacations," Tracy said, not mentioning to Regina how she thought she'd been stalked. "But I did buy a bag of fake jewels for WINOH," she added.

"Don't tell me you didn't go to a party," Regina said.

"I went to a party after I talked to you," Tracy said.

"And?"

Tracy assumed Regina wanted to know if she had met an available guy. "The party was all right." Tracy went back to her work. She decided against mentioning the man she saw at the yard sale and how she thought he stalked her and that later that evening she saw him at the party.

Tracy made another attempt to finish her work. But her mind was filled with more pleasant thoughts of Evan Maxwell.

"Tracy . . . Tracy!" Regina leaned over her desk. "Maybe I should take a weekend trip to St. Hope Isle." She grinned. "I'm glad you enjoyed yourself."

"Yes," Tracy said, taking another sip of her tea, which tasted more like lightly sweetened water now.

"So, what is his name?"

"Why do you ask that?" Tracy inquired, not sure if she should tell Regina about meeting Keith's twin. She was certain that Regina would get her chance to meet Evan eventually.

"I called your name twice before you answered."

Tracy gave her best friend her full attention.

"Oh, I didn't meet anyone on the island, at least no one that I liked." She took a sip of tea before adding, "But, I met Keith's twin brother last night at Hannah's."

"Get out of here . . . don't tell me there are two of them running around boring the city."

In spite of herself, Tracy laughed. "I don't know if he's as boring as his brother. I think he's different." Tracy picked up the pink note and read the information from the agent who had left her another message regarding the apartment.

"Does he live in the city?" Regina asked, leaning against her desk.

"Regina, I don't know."

Regina drummed her long nails against her cheek. "Is he married?"

Tracy lifted the cup to her lips and looked over the rim at her girlfriend. "I didn't see a wedding band on his finger."

"If you checked out the ring finger, he made an impression on you."

Tracy smiled. She didn't tell Regina that Evan was supposed to call her. Neither did she mention his invitation to dinner. What surprised her more was that she was anticipating his call. She rolled her chair away from her desk and stood. "I'm going to find the agent who wants to rent one of my apartments."

"Please do," Regina said. "He really needs a listing."

"Yes," Tracy replied, as she left the office to find the agent. Just as she stepped out of her office and into the corridor, she saw the agent leaving Keith's office.

"Hey, Tracy," the young man said.

"Hi, I got your message. If you want to stop by and talk to the manager, it's fine with me."

"Thanks." He reached out, giving her hand a grateful squeeze.

Tracy understood the agent's anxiety. Keith Maxwell had a policy: He expected each agent to present at least three sales, three property listings, or three property closings at the sales meeting.

"You're welcome," Tracy said.

"I have the person's name and phone number if you would like to speak to her." The agent hurried to the inner office before Tracy could stop him.

As she turned to go inside her office, she noticed Evan and Keith walking out of Keith's office. She observed how handsome Evan appeared in his dark suit as he walked toward her.

"Hi." Evan spoke, his voice smooth and so low she could barely hear him.

"Hi," she said, inhaling his heady cologne, determined not to allow the pleasant reaction at seeing him surface.

Evan touched her waist, resting his hand lightly against her. "Have lunch with me."

The warmth in his voice sent vibrations through Tracy, and she almost wanted to cancel her appointment.

"I can't," she said, forcing herself to stay in

control of her feelings. "I have an appointment."

"Evan, let's go, man." Tracy heard Keith call out to his brother.

"All right, give me a minute," Evan said to Keith. He lowered his dark head, his lips almost touching Tracy's. "We'll talk later."

She couldn't speak. She could only look into his eyes, forcing him to return her gaze, and hope he read her agreement. Her expression promised that she would have lunch with him soon. Tracy felt him release her. She regarded him with admiration as he walked out with his brother.

Tracy went to her office and sank down in her chair. Warnings sprinted through her with the caution to be careful. She accepted her inner advice, and vowed to keep her distance from the man she knew was capable of making her forget she had a job.

In a few seconds, the agent was back, standing at her desk to give her the prospective tenant's name and phone number.

"He must be excited." Regina rose from her work and looked at Tracy.

"I think so," Tracy said, recognizing the woman's name. She was from the Women in Need of Help program.

She deposited the paper in the tray on her desk and called the prospective client, confirming the appointment. "I'll see you later," Tracy said to Regina after she finished her phone conversation.

"Don't be late for the meeting," Regina called out.

"Don't worry. I'll be on time." The WINOH committee was meeting to gather ideas on how to raise money for the program, which was in desperate need of funds.

Finding a company to donate new computers and other office equipment was first on the agenda. Next, the program was in need of two instructors willing to volunteer a few hours each week to teach the business class. Much effort was needed to keep the private program functioning. Without volunteers and funds, it would be impossible for Women in Need of Help to survive.

This reminded Tracy to call Hannah, who had volunteered to donate the refreshments for tonight's meeting. Tracy hurried back to her desk and dialed Hannah's number.

"Will the refreshments be ready for tonight?" she asked her sister.

"Let me check with the chef," Hannah said.

Tracy checked her watch and waited. She should've called Hannah from her cellular on her way to her appointment. Hannah managed to hire a chef just out of culinary school. He was good but arrogant, to say the least. Tracy was sure he spread his imaginary polychromatic feathers at every opportunity.

"He'll have the food ready before the meeting," Hannah's voice cut into her musing.

"Thanks, Hannah," Tracy circled her fingers, touching her forefinger to her thumb, to gesture to Regina. She hung up and hurried out to her car.

The late-afternoon sun beamed down on Tracy, cloaking her like a wool blanket. Tracy was sure it was a hundred degrees outside.

As she walked to her car, she noticed Evan and Keith going into a building a few doors down from Maxwell Realty. She slid behind the wheel of her car, and promised herself that she wouldn't think about Evan again.

It was almost impossible to keep her mind free from thinking about him. *And why?* she mused. Evan was Keith's exact image, and she'd never looked at Keith twice, not even when he was single. When she did give her broker attention, it was to simply listen to him complain in a meeting that sales and listings were low. The other times she made contact with Keith were to pick up her commission checks.

She reminded herself again that Evan was different in ways that she couldn't exactly figure out. It never occurred to her that twins had differences and that maybe they didn't think the same.

She exited I-85, driving into an old neighborhood. She counted the numbers on the houses until she arrived at the address she'd scribbled on her notepad.

The house appeared to have been plucked from a book of fairy tales, and set among modest homes. Cream-colored cement swirled like trails through brown stones. The creamy swirls reminded her of melted marshmallows, dropped in hot cocoa on a cold winter's night.

Tracy took her briefcase and purse and got out of the car. For a moment she studied the yard and wondered how successful she would be at convincing the seller—if she chose to sell—to redo the lawn.

Brown patches spotted the dying grass. The few flowers that edged the splintered walkway drooped from lack of water. Stubborn weeds sprouted between the cement cracks. Tracy was convinced that chemicals were the only remedy strong enough to destroy the weeds.

I've been in business for a while, she mused, regarding the yard. With a little coaxing, Tracy hoped to reassure the seller that showing her property love and attention might be what she needed to expedite the sale of her home.

Tracy rang the doorbell and waited patiently for the owner to open the door.

"Mrs. Peterson?" Tracy asked.

A short, plump woman opened the door wider, lifting her glasses to her eyes. Mrs. Peterson squinted at Tracy's gold name badge that read TRACY WILSON, MAXWELL REALTY.

"Come in." Mrs. Peterson displayed a friendly smile.

"How are you today?" Tracy moved inside, surveying the congested foyer. A rose-colored, overstuffed chair positioned across from a blond, polished table made the room appear significantly smaller than its size.

"I'm feeling all right," Mrs. Peterson said, smiling up at Tracy. " I wish this weather would cool off."

"Me too," Tracy replied, looking around for

the light switch. "Mrs. Peterson, would you mind turning on the lights?" Tracy asked wanting to get a better view of the room.

"Sure," Mrs. Peterson said as she flipped the light switch for Tracy.

Tracy checked for cracks or water stains on the walls.

"How much do you think I'll get for my home?" Mrs. Peterson asked.

"We'll discuss prices as soon as I finish looking at the house," Tracy replied, not wanting to raise the woman's hopes too high. "Can we start upstairs?" Tracy asked, glancing at the thick, reddish carpet covering the stairs.

"I guess we can." Mrs. Peterson let out a sound of lament. "These old knees of mine are so bad with arthritis. I don't sleep up there anymore."

"I can look if you don't feel like climbing the stairs," Tracy offered. "It'll only take a minute."

"I think I can make it up just this once," Mrs. Peterson said. "I took my medicine this morning, and it made me feel better." She slowly climbed the stairs.

Tracy wasn't offended. She'd read how people disguised themselves as buyers and agents, entering a home with intentions to steal.

They finally reached the second floor. Three clean bedrooms with not a speck of dust impressed Tracy. She turned to Mrs. Peterson. It was as if the woman read her mind.

"I have a cleaning lady to tidy up once a week."

"I see," Tracy said and checked the bathroom, which was equally clean.

Finally, they arrived downstairs. The living room was almost perfect, with a pink, floral sofa set and lush, green ivy plants.

They moved to the kitchen. The appliances weren't new but were well cared for. Tracy made notes on her form as they entered the dining room, and sat at a long, glossy-brown table. The china closet was filled with china and crystal. Tracy assumed that Mrs. Peterson entertained and served wonderful dinners in this exceptionally nice room.

"So, you're interested in selling," Tracy said. Some sellers had a tendency to change their minds once they were seated at the table.

"I need to sell. You see, my friends have all moved to this new senior community." She paused and looked around the dining room. "After my husband died, I didn't want to sell." She smiled sadly. "I guess I was just trying to hold on to the last part of him."

Silently, Tracy agreed. She had been trying to hold on to Drake, too. She still had wedding pictures on the mantel, his truck was in the garage, and she was constantly comparing every man that she'd talked to or dated to her late husband. If Mrs. Peterson could let go, maybe she had a chance to start over, also.

"I understand," Tracy said.

"There have also been reports of robberies lately." Mrs. Peterson sounded worried. "It's not safe to live alone."

"That's true," Tracy said, thinking how she,

too, lived alone. Listening to Mrs. Peterson's compelling decision made Tracy think that she, too, should sell her home soon and buy a condo.

"Everything is pretty much okay with the house," Tracy said. "However, I *am* concerned about the lawn." She waited for Mrs. Peterson's reply and hoped that the woman wouldn't give her a hard time.

"The lawn service raised the price, so I hired a handyman." Mrs. Peterson laughed. "He didn't care for the lawn properly," she said, then added, "If you could recommend an inexpensive lawn service, I'd be grateful."

"I'll see what I can do," Tracy said, already thinking of a lawn service that she referred to many of her clients.

After giving Mrs. Peterson a price that was comparable to the other homes selling in her neighborhood, Tracy completed the contract and gave it to the woman to sign.

"Oh, I'm going to miss this place," Mrs. Peterson said, her plump fingers trembling slightly, as she signed over her property to be sold by Maxwell Realty. She gave the contract to Tracy. "You know, this neighborhood turned out a lot of successful people."

"Really?" Tracy was curious.

"Yes, this young man that you work for lived in this neighborhood when he was a young boy. He and his identical twin brother were the two most mischievous boys I ever taught in elementary school." She chuckled softly.

"They were?" Tracy smiled, surprised that Keith Maxwell hadn't always been so stuffy.

"Yes, those boys put the *M* in mischief

Tracy continued to smile. She couldn't imagine Keith doing anything to upset anyone, but she wasn't sure about Evan.

"I think I was supposed to have been teaching Keith, but there was a rumor that those twins switched classes." Mrs. Peterson laughed again. "To tell you the truth, I still don't know whether the rumor was true. But I do know one thing. Everyone in this neighborhood was glad when their father took them to live on St. Hope Isle."

"They were that bad?" Tracy asked Mrs. Peterson, who was smiling and shaking her head as if reliving the day she learned that Evan and Keith moved out of town.

"One of them was worse than the other . . . but who knew which twin was causing the havoc?" She paused. " I wonder what the other twin is doing these days?"

Tracy smiled. *He's in Atlanta doing everything in his power to ignite my buried passion,* she thought but dared not disclose this information to her client.

"Thanks for the listing, Mrs. Peterson. I'll be talking with you soon."

Four

Tracy was still smiling when she got into her car. She was more curious than ever to know more about Evan Maxwell. She recalled how Mrs. Peterson wasn't sure which twin was the terror. It could have been Keith. He certainly terrorized the agents when they didn't meet his expectations. Tracy considered her broker as she headed back out on to the main highway. Keith might be surprised to know that the agents' nickname for him was "Sergeant Maxwell." She wondered what insulting demeanor Evan unknowingly wore.

She also wondered what profession Evan had chosen. Tracy brushed away the questions reeling through her mind, to instead pay attention to the driver in front of her, who didn't seem to know which lane he wanted to drive in.

By the time she parked and got out of her car at Maxwell Realty, the sun seemed to beam down on her like a furnace. Pacing herself, she walked into the building, embracing the coolness. As she took the elevator up to her floor, she made mental notes. She had to call a lawn service for Mrs. Peterson. She definitely had to record the listing before she attended the meeting tonight. She was not returning to the office later, especially since the thief hadn't been captured. She had forgotten to put the bag of jewelry she bought in St. Hope Isle in her car to take to the meeting with her tonight. On her way to the meeting, she would have to stop at her house and get it.

This reminded her that she needed to sell her house. It was simply too big for her.

Tracy walked into her office and closed the door, noticing that her chair was facing the window. She set her briefcase and purse on the desk and wondered why it was so hard for people to stay out of her office. She reached out, attempting to swirl the chair to its proper position.

"Hi," Evan greeted her, turning in the chair to face her.

Tracy staggered back. "What the . . . What are you trying to do, give me a heart attack!"

"So, this is how you treat your visitors." He grinned.

She couldn't help but notice his beautiful, white teeth. She could just as well assume that Evan's profession was making teeth-whitening commercials.

"Neither my visitors nor my clients wait in my office uninvited," she said, determined not to show that she was pleased to have found him in her office. "What happened to the phone call?"

"I was here and decided it was better to look at you while we talked."

"Of course," Tracy said, wondering how many women Evan charmed with that line.

His laughter filled the office. "You don't believe me?"

"I'm not sure if I should. But I have lots of work to do, and I don't have time for a visit."

"It'll only take a minute," he replied, standing and moving so close to her that she could smell his cologne. An unwanted shiver raced through her, settling close to her heart.

"What do you want?" she probed, not exactly sure if Evan Maxwell was serious about anything concerning her.

"Dinner. Tonight." He spoke the words evenly, as if any answer pertaining to "no," would be inadmissible.

"I'm busy tonight."

"Hot date with the guy I saw you with today?"

"Is that how you approach all the women you hardly know . . . inquire about their personal business?"

"Only the women I like."

"I don't intend to turn into one of your statistics, Mr. Maxwell." She made an attempt to move past him, but he blocked her path. "Sorry, I'm busy tonight."

Evan moved closer to her, and she once again felt the same quaking sensation she'd experienced minutes ago. "Then I guess I'll have to call you." His firm muscular body brushed against her as he walked out of the office.

Tracy sank in her chair. She had decided to make serious changes in her life, such as eventually dating. But her plans did not include involving herself with the likes of Evan. Not only was he cocky, but he was also a flirt. She was now more certain that *he* was the twin who had wreaked havoc in Mrs. Peterson's neighborhood and classroom.

By the time Tracy had recorded her new listing with the listing service and had called an inexpensive lawn service for Mrs. Peterson's lawn, it was almost time to leave for the Women in Need of Help meeting.

Not wanting to get stuck in traffic on her way across town, she decided to leave the office, but not before she made a call to Hannah. It wouldn't surprise her if the conceited chef decided that he was too busy after all and couldn't prepare the refreshments for tonight's meeting.

"Hannah, are the refreshments ready?"

"Yes, Tracy," Hannah confirmed, easing her worry.

"Thanks." Tracy gathered her briefcase and purse and hurried out of the office. She anticipated that tonight the committee would develop some ideas to raise money for the program.

On her way out, she passed Keith's office. He sat behind his desk, the exact image of his brother. It seemed strange that, when she looked at him, she didn't get the same sensation as when she looked at Evan.

She headed out of the building, promising herself for what seemed like the tenth time that day that she was not going to think about Evan Maxwell again.

* * *

The Women in Need of Help building was located in an old house near the edge of town. The renovated house sat on a wide lot with numerous parking spaces. A handful of carpenters in town who learned about the program through advertisements had contributed their services. The carpenters had breathed life into the dilapidated house, making it appear new.

The foyer was the reception area now, appearing large because of the mirrored walls and light shades of paint. The four upstairs bedrooms were classrooms, and the living room and dining room had been turned into conference rooms and offices.

A fish pond set at the back of the land was surrounded by pines and black walnut trees. The owner of a patio-furniture store had donated several picnic tables with brightly colored umbrellas. White benches circled the tables, turning the area adjacent to the pond into an outdoor lunch area, which resembled a small park.

Tracy took the jewelry and her purse from her car and went inside, speaking to several volunteers who were standing in the foyer discussing the evening's events.

Later, Tracy went to find Janet, the director, who was in her office flipping through a stack of folders.

"Hi. I'm glad to see you." Janet looked up from her search.

"Did you invite all those people?" Tracy asked, moving further into the office.

"If placing an advertisement in the paper and

asking for donations is an invitation, I guess I did. But I never dreamed so many people would attend this meeting." Janet snatched a file from her stack. "Here it is." She held up the folder. "I wrote a proposal," Janet said, laying the thick folder aside, explaining to Tracy that several local businessmen had agreed to allocate funds to the program.

"You certainly have been busy." Tracy dropped the bag of faux accessories on the director's desk.

"If they're serious about helping us, we'll be on our way." Janet opened the bag and began pulling out fake necklaces, laying the jewelry on her desk. "It's too bad this stuff isn't real."

"I know." Tracy laughed. "If it were, we could sell it."

"The ladies should enjoy wearing this jewelry," Janet said, placing the bag in a file cabinet. "Well, I guess you and Regina will have to call me tomorrow. I have a meeting with the men I told you about." She glanced at her watch. "I have about thirty minutes to get there."

"Me and Regina?"

"Tracy, you and Regina sell houses for a living. I know the two of you can handle this meeting."

"Where are you going?" Regina walked in just in time to catch the end of the conversation.

"I won't be attending the meeting, Regina. I'm expecting good news from the two of you tomorrow."

"Tracy, you're the speaker." Regina sank

down in a nearby chair. "I'm too exhausted to say another word."

"Me?" Tracy asked, looking at Janet and then Regina.

"Please, Tracy, I can't do it tonight." Regina shook her head slowly. She seemed upset. "Listen, I got into an argument before I left work with one of the new agents Keith hired. That woman advertised in my farm area." Regina got up and stood near the door.

A smile crossed Tracy's lips. She knew how hard Regina had worked, building a clientele in that exclusive neighborhood. "You let her know that you weren't the one to play with."

"Girl, you know I informed her," Regina said as they entered the conference room, which was decorated with vases filled with snow-white and rosy-pink carnations donated from one of the volunteer's florist shops. Two large plants were on each side of the main table where Tracy and Regina sat along with two other volunteers.

"Welcome, ladies and gentlemen," Tracy said, bringing the meeting to order. "I'm proud to see such a nice turnout. All of you are aware that our program is in desperate need of your support. We are not government funded, and there are countless women who are searching for work and who need training." Tracy stopped and surveyed the faces of the prominent people in the room. "In addition to your suggestions on raising money for the program, I would also like to ask for equipment donations. We need computers and typewriters for our business classes. We also need two instructors who will volunteer to teach a few nights a week," she announced, scanning the room for willing volunteers.

A woman in front was interested in teaching one of the classes. Tracy motioned for Regina to give the woman an application. Applause filled the room.

"Thank you." Tracy said. "The floor is open for all suggestions on ideas to raise funds."

"I suggest a talent show," offered a middle-aged man in the back of the room. His suggestion was followed by a roar of laughter.

"And do what?" the man next to him asked loud enough for everyone in the room to hear.

"If he's suggesting that we sing and dance, I think the audiences would want their money back," someone said, followed by more joviality.

Tracy interrupted the merriment. "Okay, guys, let's get serious. If we want to have a talent show, let's do it."

"Right," Regina agreed, writing the suggestion on her pad.

"Look. One computer costs about a thousand dollars," said a woman seated near the back of the room.

"Yes." Tracy acknowledged the woman, who she knew owned an insurance company.

"I don't think the money we'll raise from a talent show will buy one inexpensive computer."

The sound of papers shuffling and chairs scrubbing against the floor circulated throughout the room. Many of the guests complained that the woman's suggestion was negative.

"I'm not saying that a talent show and fund-raising dinner are not acceptable," the woman continued after Tracy waved her hand, gesturing for everyone to come to order. "I'm suggesting that we contact some of these computer companies and stores and ask for donations."

"Good idea," Tracy said, "Would you like to form a committee for that particular task?"

"Yes, I will be more than willing to contact companies for equipment donations," the insurance agent agreed.

A young woman in the front of the room raised her hand.

"Yes?" Tracy asked.

"I suggest a masquerade party," she said, "and I'll be more than happy to organize the it."

"Sounds good." Tracy smiled. "Give the director a call tomorrow."

"I can donate the computers," a voice said.

While another round of applause filled the room, Tracy looked up and was stunned. She could only stare at Evan Maxwell.

"Do you have any idea how many you can donate?" Tracy finally asked after taking a moment to gather her composure.

"I'll have to get back to you on that, but I'm sure you'll get the amount you need." Evan folded his arms across his chest and smiled at Tracy.

She realized that she was staring at him and looked away. He was attractive in black pants and a half-opened, black shirt, which displayed a gold chain circling his neck against his bare skin. Tracy kept her gaze lowered. Evan had a habit of showing up unexpectedly and surprising her. She didn't particularly like surprises, especially when they interfered with her emotional comfort zone.

The meeting continued for another hour. Tracy was pleased to see those who were attending for the first time donating their time or money and suggesting additional ideas on how to foster capital for WINOH.

Finally, the meeting was over. Tracy had thanked the volunteers, said good-bye to Regina, and headed out to her car when she noticed Evan standing in the parking lot.

"Thanks for the computers." She smiled up at him, showing appreciation for his promised donation. Her curiosity was cooled now, after learning his profession. Nonetheless, another part of her curiosity was still getting the best of her.

"You're welcome."

"How did you know that I was at this particular place?"

"I stopped by Hannah's." He grinned down at her. "When I asked for you, the woman at the bar told me that you were here and she gave me the address," he said, walking with her to her car. "Do you have a problem with that?"

"Actually, I'm glad that you were looking for me," Tracy said, hoping that she wasn't giving Evan any ideas about her feelings for him. "I mean, the program really does need computers."

"I'll do anything to help," Evan stated. "I haven't had dinner. Would you like to join me?"

"I can't have dinner with you tonight," Tracy expressed clearly. She was not ready to share a meal with him.

"Come on, Tracy. I know it's not Friday night, but we have to eat."

"Evan, I really do have to get home," Tracy said. She hadn't had a break all day, and having dinner with Evan Maxwell was not on her agenda. All she wanted to do was soak in a tub filled with hot water and bubbles, followed with a good night's sleep. "Can we have dinner tomorrow night?"

"Tomorrow night." Evan smiled. "The restaurant of your choice."

"I'll see you then," she agreed, naming her favorite restaurant.

Evan slipped his arm around her slender waist, giving her a light squeeze.

"Tomorrow night around seven."

"Yes," she consented to the time, realizing that if she were a wise woman, she would've accepted his computers gracefully and forgot that she ever met Evan.

Evan leaned closer to her, his lips barely grazing hers. "Do I get an address?"

Her mind warned her to get into her car and go home. She disobeyed. She reached inside her purse, took out a pen and business card, and wrote her address on the back. "Don't be late," she teased, sliding the card into his hand.

"I'm always on time." He winked, holding her hand before he took the card from her.

His touch was warm, firm, and gentle, captivating her spirit and draining her apprehensions. Her fears of allowing herself the pleasure of enjoying another man's presence since the death of her husband dissipated into nothingness. Tracy Wilson felt strong and whole again.

"Good night, Evan." Tracy smiled up at him as he released her hand and took her car key, unlocking the door for her. She noticed that he waited until she was inside before he walked across the parking lot to his car.

As she drove out of the lot, she watched him swaggering across the parking lot through her rearview mirror. She had to be honest with herself. She liked him.

Since she had been widowed, she was finally making plans to go out with a gentleman of her choice, and not a man that Regina or Hannah thought was right for her. She'd made the perfect decision. She would dine with Evan and accept his computer donations gracefully.

After all, Evan lived on an island. She was sure that, after a few days or weeks, he would return home. She doubted that she would see him again after their dinner date. Regardless, after admitting to herself that she was interested, she refused to dismiss any deliberations concerning Evan. She savored his touch. She could almost feel his arms around her waist. The very thought of his presence swelled her heart with sensual delight. Tracy turned on to her street, finally dismissing the short time they'd spent together. *Evan is single and probably involved and not the least bit interested in me,* she decided. She had nothing to worry about. *I have no time for serious affairs of the heart, anyway,* she silently reminded herself. *And there is nothing wrong with enjoying dinner with an attractive man.*

But in her driveway, she reminded herself how wonderful it felt to dream of romantic moments. Without further hesitation, Tracy granted herself permission to wallow in stale self-pity. Drake had been the only man for her.

With that thought clicking across her mind, Tracy got out of her car and went inside. She didn't think for a moment that Evan wasn't already involved with someone. He seemed confident and sure of himself. She also admired his take-charge, straightforward attitude. She wouldn't be surprised to learn that he was engaged. She closed her front door, along with the tiny crack in her heart that she had allowed to open while she was with Evan.

Five

Evan rang Tracy's doorbell right on time, exactly as he'd promised. Tracy opened the door and invited him in, and stood admiring him. Evan's light-gray slacks coordinated with his gray shirt, making him appear casual and comfortable. It seemed to be his usual style to leave a few buttons open at the top, displaying the chain around his neck. "I'll be right back," Tracy said, going upstairs to get her purse.

Evan smiled and nodded.

"I'm ready," Tracy said after she returned. She looked as good as she felt. Her yellow dress with half the back out was perfect for the warm evening.

"Let's go get dinner," Evan said as they walked out of her house.

Tracy noticed that Evan's cheerful demeanor had vanished between the time she had gone upstairs and returned. She decided that maybe it was a part of his personality. She barely knew him and could hardly judge his attitude.

Riding to the restaurant, Tracy also noticed that Evan was quiet. However, once they arrived

and were seated at their table, he began to talk
to her.

Tracy sliced a small piece of cucumber from
her salad, eating the crispy slice slowly as she
listened to Evan speak about of his business. He
and his partner hadn't been lucky. But they'd
worked extra hard to accumulate success.

"When are you opening the store in Atlanta?"
she asked, her attention captured by the man
she'd found herself attracted to in just a short
time.

"In another few weeks," Evan said, spearing
a cherry tomato and popping it into his mouth.

"I suppose you will visit Atlanta often," Tracy
said, secretly hoping that Evan, instead of his
partner, would work in Atlanta.

"We've planned to spend a few months at a
time building this business," Evan replied.

She and Evan finished their salads seconds before the waiter set their meals before them. "So,
tell me," Evan began, while winding strands of
spaghetti around his fork. "How long have you
worked for Keith?"

"I've been with Maxwell Realty for almost three
years now," she said, remembering how she and
Drake worked together as partners at a competing firm before his death. When he died, she
could barely stand to work at the company. She'd
missed Drake so much. If she needed a question
answered or a property needed showing, and she
couldn't make the trip, he would have taken over.
But most of all, she missed his presence.

It was Drake who always argued with the broker. It was Drake. . . . She let her thought trail.

"I suppose you enjoy your work," Evan said, stopping to notice the two violinists who were now serenading a couple at the table across from them.

Tracy smiled before she answered Evan's question, watching the young lady, who seemed surprised that her lover was having her serenaded. "I really do enjoy what I do. It's a lot of competition, but that's what makes the work interesting," she said, slicing a thin piece of chicken breast and eating the tender meat.

They were quiet for the rest of their meal, only making small comments about the violinists. Tracy was surprised that she was enjoying the evening. Evan was polite and didn't seem to be the mischievous type that Mrs. Peterson had described. Then Tracy decided that maturity was part of growing up, and Evan was certainly a graceful man.

As they finished their meals, Evan poured them both another glass of wine. "Tracy, I'm sure your clients must invite you to dinner often."

"Sometimes," Tracy said, sipping the white vintage and setting the glass down. She was right. Evan wanted to purchase property, and he wanted her to find and work the deal for him. "Are you interested in buying a house or a condo?"

"Yes, but not right now," he said.

Tracy noticed the narrow gaze he gave her and couldn't figure out what he meant.

"I asked you out because I thought you were single."

"Oh—" Tracy started, but he didn't let her finish.

"I don't invite married women to dinner unless it's business. I really wanted us to be friends." He drank a short swig from his wineglass, set it down, and gave her another intense gaze. "I don't date married women.

"Evan. . . ." She started but stopped when she noticed him raise his hand.

"If I have offended you, I'm sorry."

Tracy was surprised that Evan assumed she was married. She realized that this could have been the reason for his silence earlier. Tracy proceeded to correct the misunderstanding. "You have not offended me, Evan," she said, realizing that he had seen her wedding pictures. "My husband was killed in a plane crash." She lowered her gaze, not wanting Evan to see the leftover grief that lingered in her heart.

"I'm sorry. I didn't know your husband was dead."

"You must have seen my wedding pictures. I've thought about putting them away."

"Have you always lived in Atlanta?" Evan asked, changing the subject.

"Born and raised," Tracy said, giving him a proud smile. She was aware that he'd lived in the city when he was a child and wanted to know more. "You were born here, right?"

Evan fingered the stem of his almost empty wineglass, cleared his throat, and grinned. "I was born in St. Hope Isle. From what I understand, my mom got really bored with the island,

and she and my daddy moved us back to Atlanta when Keith and I were toddlers."

"So, your mother still lives here?"

"Yes," Evan said.

"And your father?" Tracy was curious.

"My parents are divorced." Evan shrugged. "My father died a few months ago."

"Oh, I see," Tracy said, not knowing what else to say. Her father didn't have the decency to divorce her mother. He had simply run away from home.

"My parents were divorced years ago," Evan continued. "I guess the divorce was harder on me than it was on Keith." He smiled at Tracy. "But I survived."

"Your father lived in Atlanta?"

"He lived on the island." Evan took another sip of wine and set his wineglass on the table. He leaned back in his chair. "I miss him. You know."

"I understand," Tracy said, telling him that both her parents had died when she was a girl. "Hannah raised me."

Evan chuckled. "I was wondering why you work at Hannah's."

"Now you know," Tracy said, adding that Hannah was the only close living relative she had, other than two aunts. "I try to help her and Jordan out as much as I can. She has been very good to me over the years."

"From the looks of you, she treated you well." Evan chuckled again.

The waiter laid the bill on their table before she could respond.

Evan immediately looked at the bill and placed some money inside the leather binder. "Where do you want to go?" he asked her after the waiter removed the binder.

"I don't know. I'm with you," Tracy answered, almost shocking herself with her answer. If she'd been out with one of the dates that Hannah or Regina had set up, she would have told the gentleman to take her home. But Evan was different. She enjoyed being with him.

Evan pushed away from the table and stood. "We'll think of something," he said, looking at her.

Tracy grabbed her purse, and they walked out to his car. She waited patiently while Evan opened the car door and allowed her to sit.

He slid in beside her and started the engine before turning on the headlights and sliding a CD into the stereo system. He pushed the shuffle button but stopped it when a love song began to play as he drove out into the street. Tracy stole glances at him, wondering how she had been lucky enough to meet a man she liked enough to spend an entire evening with, without wanting to go home before midnight. "Do you think you'll like living in the city again?" She broke the silence as they headed further out of town.

"I don't have a problem with living here," he said, turning off the main highway and down a country road. He slowed the car and looked at her. "I enjoy being close to my family, and being with you will make my life a little easier."

"Oh, please, you're telling me that you don't

have a woman friend waiting for you on the island?"

"Believe it or not, Tracy, I don't," he answered, while driving up to a building and shutting off the engine. Evan rolled the car window down.

This was hard for Tracy to believe, since she'd noticed the women at the WINOH meeting, at Maxwell Realty, and at Hannah's admiring him.

"Come on, Evan, you can give a better answer than that," she said, not wanting to get her hopes up too high. Evan seemed to be a man that she could love. If he had a lover, she would understand. Her heart was still frazzled and in no condition to be broken.

He turned to her and leaned back, his head resting on the seat. "My last love affair ended more than six months ago," he confided. "She moved back to England."

"What does that have to do with anything?" Tracy asked, studying him. "Couples have long-distance relationships all the time."

"It's not that. I travel most of the time, and we didn't get to see each other much." He looked out toward the building they were parked in front of, as if in deep thought. "She found another lover, and that was the end of us."

"I'm sorry," Tracy said, wondering if she really was sorry, or if she was just being polite. She concluded that she was being polite, secretly thankful that Evan was a free man.

"I suspect that you have a good male friend," he said in a low, soft voice.

Tracy did have a friend but not a lover. An older man who was an agent at another office took her to lunch sometimes. Tracy mostly saw Barry when they were at conferences, or if he stopped by Hannah's for a drink or dinner. He often showed and sold a few of her listings. Barry wanted more than friendship. He was nice but not her type.

"I haven't had a serious relationship since . . ." her voice trailed off. She didn't want to discuss her feelings about Drake with Evan.

"Are you over your husband's death?" Evan asked.

With as much restraint and truthfulness as she could muster, Tracy said that Drake's death was hard for her. "I think about him," she said, hoping that Evan wouldn't pry further.

"Do you have children?" Evan inquired.

She looked straight ahead, allowing the painful memory to surface. It was like yesterday when she and Drake had planned to start their family. She looked forward to them each taking shifts, getting up at night to comfort and feed their baby. "No," she finally said, not wanting to discuss her painful memories further. "Evan, you mentioned that you wanted to talk to me about something."

"Yeah," Evan said, taking her hand in his. "I think you might have a dia—"

"Hey, Evan, what's up, man!" A man leaving the building stopped at the car and noticed Evan through the car's open window.

Evan and the man talked for a minute or two.

When he left them, Evan opened the door. "Let's go inside."

"I've never been to this place before," Tracy said, walking with him inside the building and forgetting that Evan hadn't finished telling her what he wanted to talk to her about.

"I think you'll enjoy yourself," Evan said, touching his hand to her waist as they maneuvered around the crowd and moved further inside.

Tracy was pleased with her surroundings once they entered the building. She noticed that the ceiling was as blue as the night sky and was studded with lights shaped like tiny stars. The place resembled a garden made in paradise, with lime green-covered tables, sitting between trees and flowers, along with a waterfall. Several couples were seated, while others danced. From where Tracy stood next to Evan, she could see into another room. Men and women were playing cards, while others played billiards.

"I never knew this place existed," Tracy said, surprised at Evan for knowing about the club.

"It once belonged to my daddy," he said, taking her hand and leading her out to a wide patio that was just as attractive as the club's interior.

"Who owns it now?" Tracy asked, allowing him to lead her outside for their first dance.

"Believe it or not, Tracy, my mother does." He chuckled and circled his arms around her, drawing her to him. "She rents it to a guy in town."

Evan moved slowly to the rhythm of the music

that swept her into his world. They danced until the early hours of the morning, stopping to sip lemon drinks because she and Evan both agreed they didn't want anything stronger at that hour of the morning.

Tracy couldn't remember enjoying herself as much as she had with Evan.

"I had fun," Tracy said when he parked in her driveway and turned off the car.

"I have a feeling you've had better times," he said softly as they got out of the car and he walked her to her door.

Tracy took her key from her purse and unlocked the door to her house. She and Drake had once done fun things like she and Evan had done tonight. She and Drake found out-of-the-way places and turned their evenings into perfect bliss.

"Believe me when I tell you this was fun." She smiled up at him, feeling the weight of his arm around her waist. Tracy sank against him, allowing Evan to kiss her lips lightly, causing buried passion to surface within her. Evan held her closer, as his kiss deepened.

"I'll call you," he said, smothering her lips with this promise before releasing her.

Tracy's only response was to smile. She never dreamed that she would ever meet a man that she actually liked as much as she'd liked Drake in the beginning.

Six

The next day, Tracy sat on a stool in the expediting room behind the bar in Hannah and Jordan's dinner club and waited for Regina. Since she didn't see the woman in charge, Tracy began assisting the waiters with coffee, silverware, napkins, and whatever else they needed to help speed up service for the customers. Waiters brushed passed her, taking iced tea and lemonade to the customers and yelling for pieces of flatware to give to customers who had dropped utensils on the floor.

While waiting, Tracy sampled lobster bisque and remembered her evening with Evan. It had been too many years since she'd been kissed. It was her fault, since she had never allowed her previous dates the opportunity to even hold her hand. Kissing was absolutely out of the question. With Evan, she hadn't felt like she'd been cheating on Drake. He'd made her feel free to express herself. She also didn't feel that Evan was forcing her to be his friend.

Although he promised to call her, Tracy wasn't getting her hopes up. It was all too good to be true.

"I called you last night, Miss Thing, and you weren't home." Regina's voice cut into Tracy's reflections.

Tracy couldn't control her laughter. She had finally begun to enjoy herself without Regina knowing about her plans. "I beg your pardon?"

Regina smoothed the back of her tan sundress down and slid onto a stool beside Tracy. "When I called the center last night, Janet said she hadn't seen you. I was beginning to think you had a date, girl."

Tracy dipped the spoon into the bisque and held it up to cool. "I did," she replied, letting out another chuckle.

"You did?" Regina scooted further onto the stool to get comfortable. "With who?" she asked, peering at Tracy.

"I went out with Evan Maxwell."

"Oh, my goodness. From that smile on your face, you had a good time."

"I enjoyed myself," Tracy said, not wanting to sound too excited.

"It's about time." Regina giggled, beckoning for one of the chef's assistants to pass her a cup of bisque. "So, I need details."

"I don't have any details that I want to share." Tracy tasted the bisque and sank her spoon inside the cup, still smiling.

"Tracy, does Evan have any buddies or guys he hangs out with on the island?" Regina asked.

"He has a business partner," Tracy answered. Regina had broken off her relationship with her friend almost a year ago, saying that she couldn't deal with Quincy Riley anymore. However, Tracy had thought that Regina was interested in one of the neighbors who lived in her condo building.

"I would like to meet his partner," Regina replied.

"You might get the chance." Tracy's tone was jovial as she kidded her girlfriend.

"I'll keep my fingers crossed."

Tracy changed the subject while the assistant slipped a small bowl of lobster bisque through the window to Regina. "Did Janet give the jewelry to the women?"

"To tell you the truth, I don't know. I worked late last night and didn't stop by to speak to Janet," Regina said. "But, when I called her last night, she didn't mention the jewelry."

"You need to be careful, Regina. I think the robber is still out there."

"I know, but if I didn't get that listing into the computer before midnight, Keith would have my head on a platter." She tasted her bisque, savoring the thick, creamy seafood soup. "And you know how he gets, if he thinks the real-estate board is going to fine him."

"I know," Tracy agreed with her, finishing the bisque. She got up and set the cup in the kitchen window. On her way back, she stopped and looked out into the bar area, thinking that she had just seen Evan. Tracy slipped onto her stool beside Regina, promising not to let her imagination run wild.

"At least you're going out. That's more than I can say for myself," Regina remarked.

"I thought you were seeing the guy that lived down the corridor from you," Tracy said.

"I had to stop seeing him. Every time I looked around, he was at my door, trying to get inside of my apartment."

"I thought you liked him," Tracy said.

"I liked him at first, but then he wanted to borrow money, and, Tracy, you know that turns me off."

Tracy shook her head. "I thought he worked at the bank."

"Yes, until he quit." Regina finished the bisque. "He told me that the job didn't pay enough money."

"You didn't need him," Tracy said.

"The last time I saw him, he was moving."

"He sold his apartment?"

"He lost it!" Regina replied.

"Girl, please!" Tracy slid off the stool. "I'm not hungry anymore," she said, reaching down to get her purse.

"Me neither." Regina also stood up. "I have a house to show, so I'll talk to you later. And I'm serious about knowing if Mr. Maxwell has a single, male friend."

"You'll have to ask him," Tracy replied.

"And let him know that I'm on the prowl for a man . . . never!"

Tracy laughed at Regina's comment. She leaned through the window, thanking the chef's assistant for her lunch.

After lunch, Tracy sat at her desk, making a call to the title company to assure that all of the paperwork was completed for the closing.

Her next call was to a young couple who wanted to see Mrs. Peterson's home. Tracy wanted to be certain that the couple qualified before she took them to see the house. She'd only had the listing for a short time, and Mrs. Peterson was getting anxious. She didn't want to get the older woman's hopes up, thinking that she had found a buyer for her home only to later learn that the couple didn't qualify.

Tracy managed to have a conference call with the couple while they were at work, verifying that they would be in her office no later than four-thirty that day.

She placed the receiver on the cradle and, without warning, she thought about Evan. He was the nicest man she'd met in a long time. Instead of bragging about his success, he was modest. What attracted her even more was his honesty. He didn't cut corners by saying what he didn't believe or what he thought she wanted to hear. And yet, he was tender and sweet, with passion and concern for her feelings. But, she'd promised herself that she was not going to allow herself to become too fond of him. She checked her watch; it was almost three-thirty—and he hadn't called. Maybe her date was like a sweet dream that wasn't true. But still the dream lingered long after she was awake.

At exactly four-thirty, Tracy's appointment walked into her office. The young couple, dressed for the scorching weather, seated themselves before her and passed her their financial folder.

"I assume you drove by and saw the house," Tracy said, opening the folder to check the information that the couple was sharing with her.

"We saw the house. It looks sort of old, but we'll take a look inside before we make our final decision," the young man said. He appeared to be in his early twenties. His bright eyes lit with a smile, but then he quickly returned to his serious expression.

"The price isn't bad," his wife added.

Tracy nodded and tapped the keys on her calculator, figuring their income and bank statements. "Well, you *do* qualify," she said when she'd finally finished and turned off the calculator. Tracy stood. "I think we should go."

"Yes." The young woman rose from her chair and waited for her husband to join her. They appeared anxious as they followed Tracy out of the office.

"Are you riding with me, or are you driving your car?" Tracy asked as they left the building. She knew that sometimes buyers wanted to ride alone, so they could privately discuss the property they planned to invest in.

"We'll meet you there," the young man said to her.

Tracy turned back to her office to get the key. She remembered Mrs. Peterson had told her that she was free to show the house without calling. In case she wasn't home, Tracy could still show the house. She took the key from her locked file cabinet and hurried out to her car.

While driving to Mrs. Peterson's house, Tracy tried not to think about Evan. She didn't need any distractions while she worked. She'd already thought about him more than she should.

It wasn't long before she was at Mrs. Peterson's home. Tracy was surprised to see that the house was now painted white. She would have preferred to have been notified of the changes. Nonetheless, Tracy was satisfied, since the house appeared more attractive. Added to the paint job was the freshly laid sod. The new, green grass gave a special touch to the house.

The young couple took their time looking at the living room while Tracy waited to take them to the next room. She turned when she heard a key jiggling in the lock. The door opened and Mrs. Peterson walked into the foyer.

"Hi." Tracy smiled, as Mrs. Peterson took a white handkerchief from her dress pocket and wiped beads of sweat from her forehead.

"Hi," Mrs. Peterson said, pushing the handkerchief into her dress pocket. Mrs. Peterson nudged Tracy, wanting to know what the couple was thinking.

"Mrs. Peterson, we'll know soon enough," Tracy told her when they were alone.

"I'm anxious, but don't mind me," Mrs. Peterson said, and she hurried to explain to the couple how the dining room was the perfect place for dinner parties.

Finally, the couple had scrutinized the entire house, promising to give Tracy a call the following day.

When they left, Mrs. Peterson seemed beside

herself. "Does that mean that they wanted to buy the house?"

"I'll let you know," Tracy said, hoping that she would get the sale. "But they did sound promising."

"If they sign the contract, how long do you think it will be before you can help me with the villa I plan to buy at the senior's village?"

Tracy shrugged because she didn't know. However, it wouldn't take long, considering that her client was prepared. "It depends," Tracy said, "Let's just settle things here, and we'll discuss that issue later."

With the showing completed, Tracy headed home for the day, anticipating hearing from her buyers, and getting a phone call from Evan.

Seven

Evan flew to the island the next morning to help solve a problem at his store. One of the buyers had received damaged equipment. After agreeing to replace the shipment, Evan met with the shipping company, learning that there had been an accident that had resulted in the damaged computers.

By the time he had finished with his meetings, it was late in the evening. He went to his office to call Tracy. He'd promised himself that, after their dinner date, he would take things slow with her. When he had waited for her in her house while she went upstairs, he noticed her wedding pictures on the mantel. He automatically assumed that Tracy was married. When she told him that her husband was no longer alive, he believed that she hadn't gotten over him. To Evan, this was a problem. He wouldn't compete with a dead man for her affections.

He also noticed that she seemed sad when he asked if she had children. It appeared that he'd struck a nerve, and at that moment a small voice warned him to *take it easy and move at a snail's pace*. But he didn't listen. He walked with her to the door, and, before he could stop himself, he had her in his arms to kiss her. *She felt good in my arms,* Evan mused, as if she were in her rightful place with him. Her body was firm against his, her lips soft and sweet. It took all of his strength to walk away that night.

Evan dialed Tracy's telephone number and waited for her to answer the phone. After several rings, the answering machine picked up. "Tracy, I had an emergency, and I had to return to the island. I'll be in Atlanta as soon as I'm finished here." He dropped the receiver back on its cradle, and reached inside his desk drawer for the extra bottle of eye drops he kept at his office.

Evan's eye began to feel strained. His eye injury was partly his own fault. If he hadn't been riding with Frank Johnson and Frank's uncles that night, he would not have been with the men when they attempted to rob a boat which turned out to be his father's boat. The men on Evan's father's boat refused to give up the goods and a fight broke out. Evan let the remembrance of his childhood fade, and he reached into his pocket, taking out a soft black case. He removed the patch and covered his eye, relieving the strain. He took his attaché case, and was just about to leave when he heard a commotion coming from Grant's office down the hall.

"Please! You can't do this to us, Mr. Lacount." Evan heard the disheartened sound of the woman's voice floating from the opened office door.

"Don't worry," Grant said to her. "We're not closing this business."

"I don't know," an older man spoke up. "We heard that you were going out of business on the island and moving to Atlanta, Georgia."

"We *are* opening a new office in Georgia, but it won't affect your job," Evan said, as he entered Grant's office, reassuring the few employees who had stayed late that their jobs were secure at Maxwell and Lacount Computers.

"Things will remain the same," Evan said. "One of us will be in and out of here as usual."

"But I worry. I have to take care of my family," the woman said, her voice piercing the room, and bringing others into the office who had heard that a meeting was taking place after work.

"Look, we're *not* closing the business." Grant held up his hand.

"The business is closing?" A male employee hurried into the room, joining the group.

"Wait . . . stop!" Evan intervened. "Where did you get this information from?"

The employees looked at each other. A woman spoke up.

"Mary told us that she heard that you and Mr. Lacount were moving."

Evan and Grant looked at everyone. "As I said before, your jobs are safe." Evan said, dismissing the group.

"You see, this is what happens when people spread rumors," one woman said to another as they left the office. "I told you not to listen to anything she says."

"I'll see you tomorrow," Evan said to Grant who was leaving to go home. His day had been a long, tedious one. A few laps in the pool, dinner, and a cool drink were what he needed to calm his nerves. "Oh, yeah, Grant. I'll need you to come to Atlanta with me on my next trip. I want you to meet the employees."

By the time Evan got home, it was too late for a swim. He poured himself a tall glass of spring water over crushed ice and listened to his messages. While he clicked off one message after another, his doorbell rang.

"What do you want, Frank?" Evan stood in the doorway, not allowing his ex-pirate friend inside the apartment.

"I'm here to pick up that package," Frank announced, pushing his hands down in the back pockets of his oversized khaki pants.

"I didn't get it," Evan said, remembering how he had been interrupted when he was about to speak to Tracy about the jewelry.

"You listen to me, Evan. If you don't take care of it, I will," Frank warned him.

Evan knew how vicious Frank could be. "Don't do anything that you'll regret, Frank. I promised you that I would return the necklace to you."

"Make it soon, or you're going to have more problems than you care to deal with." Frank turned on his heels and walked down the hall to the elevator.

Evan closed the door and wondered how

Frank had gotten into his secured building. But he was dealing with Frank Johnson, who entered where he wanted, with no keys or passwords.

Evan went back to listening to his messages. After realizing Tracy hadn't returned his call, he went to his room and called her again. When he didn't get an answer, he lay across the bed and thought about her.

Tracy needed time. Maybe he should give her space. If he pressured her, she would probably not want to see him again. He could wait, for a while. To Evan, Tracy was worth waiting for.

Eight

The young couple had signed the contract to buy Mrs. Peterson's house by the end of the week. Tracy finished the paperwork and called Mrs. Peterson, giving her the good news.

"When can we talk about my new place?" Mrs. Peterson asked, excited.

"I'll see what's available in that area and get right on it," Tracy said before hanging up and turning to her computer and checking the available listings in the senior's community.

By the time she finished studying the listings, it was noon. Tracy got her purse and hurried out to keep her promise of visiting with Hannah, who had been upset last night when Tracy called her. While Tracy had tried to calm her sister down, she had received another call. She ignored the buzz prompting her to answer and later she learned from her caller ID that the call was long distance. She wondered if Evan had tried to call her. She dismissed the idea. It was probably Regina. She was out of town, visiting her mother.

Tracy hurried out of the building and was standing at Hannah's front door fifteen minutes later, ringing the doorbell. It wasn't like her sister to be upset. To make matters worse, Hannah hadn't mentioned to her exactly what she was upset about. She only told her that she would give her the details when Tracy came over.

Tracy rang the bell twice. When Hannah didn't open the door, Tracy used her key to let herself in. "Hannah?" Tracy called out as she walked inside. The foyer was quiet. Tracy scanned the living room. The room was clean, beautiful, and unruffled, as usual. The cream living room set looked as if it had just arrived from the furniture store. "Hannah?" Tracy stood at the foot of the stairs.

Just before Tracy was about to worry that something seriously was wrong, she went out on the back porch and found Hannah sitting on the swing. Her long legs were stretched out on the small patio serving table, and her eyes were closed.

"Wake up, lazy bones," Tracy teased, sitting next to her on the swing.

"Hi, Tracy." Hannah opened her red-rimmed eyes and ran a hand over her tangled, short hair, which looked as if she hadn't combed it all day.

"What's wrong?" Tracy asked, upset, because she'd only seen Hannah in such a state once— when their mother had died.

"I'm going to kill him." Hannah rose and folded her arms across her flat stomach.

"Who?" Tracy implored, confused by her sister's statement. She'd never known Hannah to want to harm anything or anyone, except the neighbor's rabbit, who got out and ate her herbal garden one year. Even then, she hadn't been in the condition she was in now.

"Jordan. That bastard!"

Tracy opened her mouth to speak in her brother-in-law's defense. Instead, she decided to wait and hear what Hannah was talking about. "What did he do?"

Hannah covered her face, and Tracy knew she was trying to keep her from seeing her tears. "He's having an affair."

"Oh, no!" Tracy remembered seeing him dressed in some of his best clothes. "But Jordan wouldn't do that. . . ." Tracy began, then allowed the thought to slide from her mind without pondering it further.

"Oh, yes." Hannah corrected Tracy.

"How do you know he's having an affair, Hannah?"

Hannah reached inside her shorts pocket and took out a note, which she'd copied from Jordan's cellular phone message, and handed it to Tracy. "If this isn't proof, I don't know what is." She sniffed.

Tracy read the message, which reminded Jordan that he should meet some woman at her home instead of their usual hotel room, and they would continue from where they left off. Tracy read the address.

"Hannah, maybe this isn't what it seems to be."

"Of course it is," Hannah said between tears.

"Did you speak to Jordan about this?" Tracy

asked, halfway surprised that her brother-in-law would look for love in other places. Hannah was still attractive at forty-two years old. She still had her figure, even after she had her son Shun, nineteen years ago. The only reason that she kept her hair cut short was because it was easier to care for.

"I asked him, and of course he had no idea what I was talking about, so I made him sleep out here"—she waved her long, delicate fingers—"on the porch."

"Hannah, I think you need to talk him and not throw him out."

"He's meeting this woman tonight, and I need you to come with me."

"Oh, no." Tracy protested, not wanting to get involved with her sister's problems. If Jordan were having an affair, she didn't want to see it. And if he wasn't, she and Hannah were going to look foolish. "Maybe he's doing something to surprise you," Tracy said, hoping that her sister would change her mind.

"I'm truly surprised." Hannah stood up. "I gave that man the best years of my life, and how does he repay me?"

"I really don't want to go with you."

"Fine, don't go. I'll go alone."

"Okay," Tracy said after visualizing Hannah getting into trouble. Going with her would be better than bailing her out of jail. "I'll go with you." Tracy knew her sister. She was stubborn enough to find Jordan, and who knew what would happen to him or her.

"He's supposed to be there at seven." She sat back on the swing. "You can ride with me."

Tracy got off the swing. "I'll see you tonight," she promised and left her sister sitting on the back porch.

As she drove over to Hannah's dinner club Tracy still couldn't visualize Jordan having an affair. She simply couldn't believe it. *I pray that Hannah is wrong in her speculations,* Tracy thought as she waited in her car for Hannah to leave the club that evening.

When Hannah walked out to her car, Tracy got out and joined her. "Hannah, when you find Jordan, please don't start a scene."

"I need to see for myself," she said, slamming the car door so hard that Tracy feared the window would break.

Hannah drove out into the street, squealing the tires as she turned the corner and almost hit an oncoming car.

"Please slow down," Tracy said, securing her seat belt as they whizzed by stores and shops and cars at high speed.

"Hannah, if you don't slow down, you're going to get a ticket, and you'll miss Jordan altogether," Tracy said, hoping that Hannah had enough sense to fear getting a ticket.

Hannah slowed down, and from that point on, she drove at normal speed until they reached their destination.

Hannah was out of the car and ringing the woman's doorbell before Tracy could get out.

Tracy decided to wait in the shadows, while Hannah waited for the woman to open the door.

"I'm here to speak to Jordan," Tracy heard Hannah tell the woman after she opened the door.

"I'll get him," the woman said.

Tracy could hear music playing in the background and noticed that the woman was wearing small, tight white shorts, a short blouse that showed her midriff, and black sneakers with white socks rolled down to her ankles.

Tracy also noticed that it took Jordan less than two minutes to get to the door.

"Hannah! Why can't I ever surprise you with anything?"

"What surprise?" Tracy heard Hannah say. Her voice sounded as if she had been crying again.

"I'm taking dance lessons."

"Lessons?"

"I wanted to dance with you on our anniversary, Hannah." Jordan sounded disappointed that Hannah had spoiled the surprise with her distrust.

"I'm sorry," Hannah apologized.

"Would you like to join me, Hannah, and be my partner?" Jordan offered, holding out his hand to her.

At that moment, Tracy was glad that Jordan couldn't see her. She was also glad that Jordan had been faithful.

"No," Hannah said, "I'll see you when you get home."

Tracy knew she should've driven her car. "Are you ready to go?" Tracy asked her.

Without saying a word, Hannah got into the car and drove Tracy back to the dinner club.

Once they were in the parking lot, Tracy turned to her sister. "Now, don't you feel foolish?"

Hannah didn't look at her. She got out and thanked Tracy for going with her. "I have never been so embarrassed in all my life," she said. "Jordan started going out once a week when I began this semester at school. I was so sure he was having an affair."

"I think Jordan is in this marriage to stay, Hannah." Tracy comforted her, meaning every word.

"I'll try to stop by tomorrow after the antique sale," Tracy said, going to her car.

As she drove home, she wondered if Evan had kept his promise to call her.

She understood that he was a busy man. But she did notice that he carried a phone in his pocket. She turned off the main highway. Maybe it was better if she forgot Evan.

Ten minutes later, she was home. She went to her room to listen to her phone messages. She pressed the numbers to her voicemail on the telephone. Instead of being able to access her messages, the recorded voice refused to allow her entry. The recording reminded her that her code was wrong. Without wasting time, Tracy called the telephone company and learned that the phone service in her area was having problems.

It doesn't matter if the services aren't operating properly, Tracy thought. It was clear that Evan wasn't interested in her. If he was, he would've kept his promise and called her cellular.

Nine

The white mansion sat behind tall, green pines and rose up from a thick, manicured lawn. The sweltering morning heat shifted to a cooler temperature. Honeysuckle scented the air, mingling with fresh, damp dew. The mist began to evaporate from the rising sun.

Tracy climbed the wide steps leading to the steel-blue porch. This was Keith's exclusive listing, and he wanted to show the mansion, which included both modern and antique furniture, to all his agents. According to Keith, he needed the agents geared up to help him sell it. It wasn't that Keith needed help. It was Keith's habit to invite the agents.

This was one of the things Tracy liked about Keith. He also invited them to purchase some of the antiques. Initially, Tracy was interested in purchasing an antique iron bed. But lately, she'd played with the idea of selling her house and buying a condo. She didn't want antiques in her condo. However, changing her mind didn't lessen her interest in the iron bedroom set upstairs.

Tracy climbed the stairs, her short, white dress moving with her hips as she walked to the room on the second floor where an agent told her that she'd seen an iron bed. Tracy walked down the long hallway, stopping briefly to browse in the other bedrooms until she found the room with the iron-post bed.

The room was large and dark. Gangly ginger chiffonniers—a dresser and chest—stood in the room like apparitions from the past. Even the lamps on the matching nightstands were dark and eerie. Tracy crossed the room to open the thick, dark velvet drapes, and then she felt arms around her waist, twirling her around. A scream caught in her throat as lips covered hers. The kiss was strong and hungry.

"Evan!" Tracy caught her breath when he finally raised his dark head.

He responded with another ravishing kiss. As his lips searched and explored. Tracy felt her heart pound, demanding more, until he finally backed away from her.

"Can we get out of here?" he asked, drawing her toward the door.

"Not now," Tracy finally said. She understood that Keith disliked the agents leaving in the middle of viewing one of his listings.

"I'll talk to Keith," Evan said, walking with her out into the hallway. "He'll just have to understand that I'm hungry and I need you to have lunch with me."

"I doubt he'll excuse me for that reason," Tracy said, trying not to let Evan distract her further while they went to find Keith.

They found Keith at the edge of the stairs. "I'm going to lunch," Tracy said to him.

"With him?" Keith joked, referring to Evan.

"The man said he was hungry." Tracy folded her hand in Evan's. "You wouldn't deprive him of a meal, would you?" Tracy asked, not giving Evan a chance to make excuses for her leaving early.

Keith grinned. "I'll see you next week, Tracy."

"Thanks, Keith," Evan said.

Tracy slipped her arm around Evan's waist and walked with him out of the house. "I'll follow you to the restaurant," she said, stopping at her car.

"I don't have a car," Evan replied." I guess I'll have to bum a ride with you." Evan gave her a pleading gaze. "At least until I can rent a car."

"I guess I can give you a ride," Tracy teased him. "Considering that I haven't seen or heard from you until today."

"If you listen to your messages, you would've known that I was in St. Hope Isle."

Tracy got in and unlocked the door for Evan. "I—" she started to protest and then remembered that her phone service had problems. "My phone had a problem."

"I didn't know what to think," Evan replied, sliding in beside her.

"Where are we going?" Tracy asked Evan once they headed back into town.

"To my hotel, where we can have lunch." He paused. "If it's it okay with you."

"It's fine with me," Tracy replied. "But why can't we go to a restaurant?"

"I need to talk to Grant."

"Grant?" Tracy gave him a sideways glance, trying to keep her eyes on the road.

"He's my partner," Evan said, leaning back against the seat to get comfortable. He reached in his jacket pocket and pulled out a small cigar, peeled off the cellophane, and stuck the beige, plastic holder between his teeth.

"I hope you don't think you're smoking that thing in here," Tracy said, pressing the brake, preparing to put Evan out if he lit the cigar.

"I like chewing the tip," Evan said.

Tracy didn't comment. As long as he just chewed the plastic holder, she would listen to Evan's reason for the habit.

"I only do this when I'm thinking," he said, settling against the seat.

"Are you having problems, Mr. Maxwell?" Tracy inquired in a teasing tone.

"I had an emergency back home," Evan said. "I had to leave without telling you."

"Is everything all right?" she asked, hoping that he didn't have to leave soon this time.

"Things are in order now."

"How long will you be in town?" she asked, knowing she should wish he would board the next flight back to the island and never return. She was in no condition to love again. However, she couldn't resist the promising affection and tantalizing effects Evan had on her.

"I'll be here for a few days," Evan promised, reaching out and pressing his hand to her thigh.

Tracy shuddered under his sensual touch. "Don't do that."

"Why?" He spoke softly.

"It disturbs my concentration while I'm driving."

He inched his hand further.

Without another warning to him, Tracy slowed and pulled over to the curb. "If you don't behave yourself, you can take a bus to the hotel."

Evan grinned and laid his arm across the back of the seat. "I wouldn't want you to have an accident because you can't stand the touch of my hand. . . ." He stopped talking and laughed.

Tracy assumed that he thought her heated glance was supposed to be a laughing matter. "Wise cracks like that are a sure way to get you put out of the car and waiting on a bus," she stated, not admitting that Evan's caress kindled a tiny yet warm blaze near her heart.

They finally reached the hotel and ordered lunch. The dining room was quiet, except for a few muffled conversations taking place among the people seated at three other tables. Contemporary music filled the room, and laughter occasionally floated out to them.

Tracy sat across from Evan, puzzling over whether or not they could actually have a serious love relationship. When she first met him, he wanted to talk to her. Tracy was sure now that Evan had been flirting with her. But just for the fun of it, she decided to ask him again.

"Evan, how long are you going to make me wait before you tell me whatever it was that you wanted to talk to me about?"

Evan appeared serious. He reached across the

...le and covered her hand with his. "While you were on the island. . . ." He looked past her and out into the dining room and stopped speaking. Tracy turned to see what had gotten Evan's attention. She noticed a tall man dressed in light-colored slacks and shirt walking toward their table. His complexion was a half a shade darker than Evan's, and his hair was as thick, black, and wavy as Evan.

"Hi." He spoke to Evan, and then turned to Tracy.

"Grant, this is Tracy Wilson," Evan said.

"Hello," Tracy replied. It seemed that Grant wanted to talk to Evan. Tracy pushed away from the table. "Excuse me," she said, taking her phone from her purse. "I have to make a call. I'll be right back." She left the men to their meeting.

It took only a few minutes for Tracy to complete her phone call. She stuck the phone inside her purse, and it dawned on her that she had never told Evan that she had been on the island. Keith may have told him. Tracy mused over the idea while walking back to the table, and then she saw Regina seated at a table not far from her table.

"Regina, what're you doing here?" Tracy was surprised to see her.

"One of my clients was in town, and she wanted me to stop by her suite. And you?" Regina leaned her head to one side.

"Evan is staying here, and we were about to have lunch," Tracy said. "Matter-of-fact, his partner is in town. Why don't you come over and meet him."

"Tracy, that's a good idea," Regina said, getting up from her table. "I wonder if I will like him," she said, walking with Tracy.

"I don't know if you'll like him or not."

"I hope so. And I hope he's not crazy or lazy or . . ."

"Regina, will you stop?" Tracy said as they neared her and Evan's table.

"Regina, this is Evan." Tracy smiled and introduced Evan Maxwell. "And this is Grant Lacount."

"Hello," Regina said to the men, and she smiled at Grant.

"Grant, would you and Regina like to join us?" Tracy asked. It was her time to play matchmaker. She smiled at Regina.

"If Regina doesn't mind, I'll get a table for us," Grant said.

"I have a table, and you're welcome to have lunch with me," Regina remarked gingerly.

Tracy noticed Evan's smile as Regina and Grant walked over to Regina's table. "Matchmaker." Evan chuckled.

"No!" Tracy laughed in spite of the truth.

The waiter set their food on the table. She and Evan made modest conversation. Tracy ate her salad while stealing secret glances at Evan, who was devouring a thick pastrami sandwich, only stopping to wash the food down with tall glasses of iced tea.

"Tracy, I really would like for us to be good friends," Evan said, taking a break from eating.

"Evan, as much as I would like to move forward with my personal life, I'm not sure if I'm ready to open up to anyone right now." Tracy tried to make him understand. It wasn't that she didn't like him. That was *her* problem. She liked him *too* much. However, she wasn't sure if she could handle a sentimental friendship. She was ambivalent. If she and Evan were more than friends, could she love him as he would expect, or would she find herself comparing him to Drake? What if she fell in love with him and their long-distance love affair didn't work out? Tracy's insecurities were mounting every second, outnumbering her sound judgment.

"I'm not going to tell you that I have time to wait, because I don't believe in waiting," Evan warned.

Tracy noticed that his gaze was fixed on her, grazing her with charcoal-gray eyes.

"I'm not asking you to wait or to understand my feelings. . . ." She paused, taking in his handsome features. "I'm just not sure I'm ready."

"How would you know if you're ready or not, if you're not willing to let it happen?"

"And if I do, and it doesn't work out because I'm not satisfied?"

"You'll never be satisfied as long you compare me to your husband, Tracy."

"I'm not . . ."

Evan gave her a look that made her aware that she wasn't deceiving him, as if he knew that she was comparing him to her late husband. Tracy was a determined woman. She decided to store her love for Drake away in her heart. He was gone and would never return to her. She would allow Evan to unleash the passion threatening to escape when she was in his presence or when he touched her. Tracy made up her mind; she had nothing to lose.

They finished their lunch in silence and spoke only when Evan was ready to go to his hotel room and change his clothes.

Once they were alone in his hotel suite, Evan gathered Tracy in his arms, exploring her lips with electrifying kisses. She returned his kisses, which aroused him with lingering passion, making both their hearts pound from sweet ecstasy.

"I love you," Evan said, planting kisses on the hollow of her neck and slowly returning to her lips, burning her with hungry obsession.

Unable to control the exhilarating currents racing through her, Tracy threw caution to the wind. The passion Evan roused within her also alerted her as to how lonely she was. She realized how she'd starved herself from intimacy. "I love you, too," she heard herself say as she unbuttoned his shirt and eased it down over his broad shoulders. She slowly unsnapped his slacks and unzipped them, her fingers slightly grazing his masculinity. He let out a low growl and unzippered her dress. Without speaking, they made their way to the bedroom, stopping to savor the sweetness of each other's lips and basking in adoration and affection. They did not stop to worry about the heap of clothing they left on the floor. They thought only of themselves and the ardent emotions that had been stirred up in each other.

Tracy allowed Evan to guide her, lowering her to his queen-sized bed and nuzzling her lips with his. At the same time, he held her in his arms, touching her spine with his fingers. Tracy felt as if her blood had turned to hot liquid and was inching through her veins. When she could stand no more, Evan stroked her inner thighs until she responded with low murmurs in sweet, sheer delight. He stopped and went to a small black case for a small foil packet. Tracy watched as he covered himself to protect her.

Unabashedly she rose to meet him, allowing sizzling iron to sink against her softness. Tracy and Evan explored and ventured into uncharted territory and roamed into unfrequented turf, sinking into and awakening each other's souls until they swirled into a sweet reservoir, where everything in their world was genuine and nothing else mattered.

Later that night Tracy awoke to the sound of Evan speaking to someone on his cellular phone. From the bed she saw him standing near the bedroom door, whispering into the receiver not loud enough for her to understand what he was saying. She looked at the clock on the night stand. It was almost eight-thirty P.M. She was about to get up when she heard Evan's whisper raise to a level she could hear and understand.

"I told you that I would take care of Tracy." She stayed still when she heard her name.

Evan was going to take care of her? Fear reached into her heart with cold, icy hands. How had she been so irresponsible as to make love to a man that was out to destroy her?

"No, I didn't tell her, but I will." Tracy continued to listen to his end of the conversation.

"I'll talk to you later, and don't call me anymore." She heard Evan hang up.

Tracy waited until she thought that Evan was asleep before getting out of bed and taking a shower. Her intentions were to sleep over, but after learning that Evan was a dangerous man, she chose to go home.

Tracy stepped out of the shower, wrapped herself in a huge, white towel, and headed to the living room for her clothes. She slipped into her dress and shoes. Out of habit, she hurried back to the bathroom to throw the towel in the hamper.

She passed his dresser and noticed a small, black note pad laying open. Out of curiosity, she peeked at the information, which confirmed her suspicions. Her name, where she worked, and who she worked for were scribbled on the pad.

Damn! Tracy thought, her apprehension tightening the muscles in her stomach. Her fear escalated as she read the information. Underneath, she read the instructions FIND THIS PERSON AND TAKE CARE OF IT.

She felt herself shivering as if her blood was laced with ice. Her teeth felt on edge, and she wanted to scream. Tears welled in her as her fear of Evan began to grow stronger with each passing minute. She had been starved for affection, and she had allowed herself to fall into a trap with a man that had been sent to hurt her. It all made sense now. Evan wanted something from her, but it wasn't love—she was sure of that. Tracy eased away from the dresser, inching toward the bedroom door. She didn't want to believe that Evan was the bad twin. But she had been right when she had imagined that Evan was the terror of the twins. She wiped a tear that rolled freely.

"Tracy?" Evan called out to her.

She felt her heart leap into her throat at the sound of her name. She froze in her tracks but didn't respond. Instead she went to the bathroom and turned on the light, casting a dim glow into the bedroom. Tracy saw Evan move to the side of the bed where she had slept. When she got up she thought he was asleep.

"Don't leave, Tracy," he said, drowsily, and she watched him sit up.

Determined to stay in control of her anger and fear, Tracy forced herself to stay calm as she walked out of the bathroom and hurried toward the door. She promised herself that she would never see Evan again.

"Tracy?" She heard him behind her now.

"I have to go," she said, turning to watch him.

"What's wrong?" he asked. In her fear, his voice seemed to come from another place, not from the man she thought she loved.

"Nothing." She continued to head for the door—and out of his reach.

"Tracy."

She felt Evan's hand on her arm.

"I'm leaving, Evan. Take your hand off me."

"No. I want to know what's going on," he said with such authority that Tracy stood back and looked at him.

"I thought we could be friends," Tracy said. She was crying now, and afraid that Evan was going to hurt her. "But after I heard your phone conversation. . . ." Her voice faded when Evan reached for her.

"I can explain," he said, his hand covering her wrist, as he pulled her to him.

"Get away from me!" Tracy screamed through sobs, struggling to loosen his grip on her wrist.

"Tracy, listen to me." He grasped the side of her waist, holding her.

"Take your hands off me!" she cried while beating Evan on his chest with her fists. "Stop holding me! Stop!" She continued to slam her fists against his chest, screaming and crying until he released his grip on her waist.

She opened the door. "Stay away from me!" Tracy hurried to the elevator. She had been right: Drake was the only man for her. It didn't matter that Evan had made love to her, allowing her to experience a sense of wholeness again. It didn't matter that she'd enjoyed him. Nothing but her safety mattered anymore.

Tracy couldn't believe that Evan had the audacity to say he loved her. And she thought that she loved him. But she *did* love him, and that was the problem. She rushed from his hotel suite, not bothering to close the door behind her.

Tracy stepped into the elevator, colliding into Grant. She turned away from him, not wanting Evan's partner and friend to see her tears. When the elevator's door finally slid closed, she was alone and allowed herself the freedom to sob.

Ten

"What's going on, Evan?" Grant asked, walking through Evan's open door.

Evan didn't answer right away. He finished pulling on his pants and hooking the snap. "Tracy overheard a conversation I was having on the phone with Frank." He was certain that Tracy thought he wanted to hurt her after listening to the phone conversation.

A curse slipped from Evan's lips. Why hadn't he told her? There had been too many interruptions, even though he had intended to tell her later that night.

"You're going to let Frank get the best of you yet," Grant said.

"I have to find her and explain," Evan remarked, putting on his shoes and grabbing his shirt from the floor. He couldn't let anything come between them. He loved her and couldn't lose her. Evan slipped into his shirt and reached for the phone, then realized that she wouldn't be home. In his rush, he couldn't remember her cellular number. He called her home number anyway and left a message on her voicemail.

"What're you doing here, anyway?" Evan

asked Grant, as he set the receiver back on the cradle. "I thought you were out with Regina."

"We went out. But we were both tired, and Regina has to work tomorrow." Grant looked at Evan. "I was going to my room when I saw Tracy at the elevator. Your door was open, so I stopped to see if everything was all right."

"I can't believe I let this happen," Evan said, raking his fingers over his hair.

"I hate to remind you, but I told you to call the police when Frank asked you to do him a 'favor,' " Grant said, shaking his head.

"Grant, I don't want to hear it," Evan said, gazing at the phone.

"Is there anything you want me to do?"

"No," he replied, not looking at Grant. "My only concern is to find Tracy and give her an explanation. It's as simple as that."

"I'll see you later," Grant said as he left.

"Yeah," Evan replied. Without further hesitation, he went downstairs and hailed a cab.

"Hannah's dinner club," Evan said to the cab driver. The dinner club was closer than Tracy's home from the hotel. She may have gone to visit her sister. If she wasn't with Hannah, he would try her home. It didn't make any sense to check Regina's place, because he didn't know her address. Nevertheless, he would find Tracy Wilson, and pray that she understood he had no intentions of hurting her.

Evan settled back into the cab and tried to relax—which was impossible. He had almost allowed his life to be destroyed once before, but with a little luck and help from his father, he had escaped. He wouldn't allow the woman he loved to get away from him because of his past.

The cab stopped in front of the dinner club. Evan paid the driver and walked across the parking lot, hoping to see Tracy's car. He didn't see any sign of it as he wove his way through rows of parked cars on his way to the club.

Once inside, he headed to the bar and sat on a stool, scanning the area for her. Couples in love sat at tables in the dining room. Evan imagined that they were whispering sweet nothings to each other. He wanted nothing more than to whisper sweet words to Tracy. He turned his attention back to the bar and tried to enjoy the soft, romantic music filling the room, his hopes of Tracy visiting her sister dissipating.

"Can I help you?" Betty asked Evan.

"White wine." Evan placed his order with the woman he'd seen working with Tracy the first night he saw Tracy at Hannah's. She placed his drink before him and turned to her next customer while Evan strained to see who was behind the window in another part of the restaurant.

While he didn't see Tracy, he looked toward the woman who had served him, motioning for her to come over. "Have you seen Tracy tonight?" he inquired, hoping she would tell him what he wanted to hear.

"No, I haven't seen Tracy tonight," Betty said. "Would you like to leave a message for her?"

At first Evan thought he would ask the woman to have Tracy call him, but on second thought he doubted that Tracy would call, since she'd been so afraid earlier.

Evan took a drink of wine and reached for his cellular, but then he remembered that he'd forgotten it. "Can I use your phone?" he asked.

"Yes." Betty set a portable phone on the counter.

Evan gave her a nod and dialed Tracy's number. She answered his call on the second ring.

"Tracy—" He heard the phone click softly. He held the receiver for a second before giving the phone back to Betty.

He could no longer deny his love for Tracy. It was strange because he was never quick to fall in love. But he knew Tracy was the woman for him. And now, he stood the chance of losing her. He couldn't let that happen.

Evan finished his drink and went outside, hailing another cab to the rental car station. As soon as the rental transaction was complete, he drove to Tracy's house, got out, and rang her doorbell.

He knew she was home; the lights were on all over the house. When she didn't appear, he finally gave up and went back to the hotel.

As he drove through the thick Atlanta traffic, Evan realized that he had been lonely until he met Tracy Wilson. Her very presence made him happy. Now he was experiencing the threat of bitter defeat, and he settled back. He was a fighter, and he didn't lose much—at least not the things that mattered most to him. If he explained to Tracy about the "favor" he'd promised to do and she still didn't want him, he wouldn't force himself on her. But he prayed that she would understand.

Eleven

Tracy sat at her computer, searching the Internet. It had been a week since she'd seen or heard from him. He'd had the nerve to call her, and he'd come to her house. Tracy shut out these irritating deliberations and continued her search, pulling up condos and penthouses on the real-estate Web site.

She spent the entire evening searching the Web for a condo that was suitable for her. Tracy wanted three bedrooms and two bathrooms and lots of space. She found what she was looking for from one of Barry's listings.

Tracy called Barry. Even though it was the weekend, she wasn't taking any chances that someone might sign a contract on the place she wanted to buy before Monday morning.

Tracy was lucky. Barry answered his pager. He was an excellent selling agent from another office. They had worked together, selling each other's listings throughout the years. Barry agreed to show her the apartment within the hour. And if she wanted, he would draw up a contract for her that same evening.

"I thought you didn't work on a Saturday night." Tracy chuckled into the receiver.

"I don't, but for you, I'll work." Barry joined her in her laughter.

"I'll see you shortly." She was pleased that she wouldn't have to spend the entire evening alone, recalling the last weekend she'd spent with Evan.

Tracy showered and changed from her cut-off jean shorts and halter into a cool, blue, summer dress and bareback heels. When she finished dressing, she made sure the doors and windows in her house were locked, safe, and secure before she went to the garage for her car. Once again, she reminded herself to buy or make a sign to advertise Drake's truck for sale. At the same time, Tracy brushed away the awakening experience she had allowed herself to feel with Evan. She told herself that she couldn't be in love with him. She would find another chore to help her forget about him, and her life would move forward. Evan was like a phantom in the night. He'd purposely intruded on her space, stole her passion, and unlocked a part of her heart that she had promised to keep closed forever.

Tracy headed over to the condo, pledging to be careful with her emotions—and of men like Evan who didn't think for one minute that her feelings mattered. She assured herself that Evan's thoughts were only of his own selfish needs. From the phone conversation she had overheard, she assumed that he had been sent to take something away from her.

A strange fear ripped through Tracy as she thought of the man who had followed her while she was on St. Hope Isles. She didn't know if Evan was connected to this man or not.

Had the phone call been from the same man that was at the hotel party?

Mrs. Peterson was right when she had described Evan. *Only now his mischievousness has made an about face to plain cruelty,* Tracy decided.

The condo on the fourteenth floor was the exact image of Tracy's dreams. She had once sold one of these condos apartments and her intention had been to purchase one of the units if she ever decided to sell her home. The bedrooms were spacious, with thick, cream-colored carpet. A long, wide balcony extended from the master bedroom, overlooking the pool and tennis court. The living room's balcony overlooked the city. A long, circular stairway led to the second floor. The island, eat-in kitchen was large, leading to a medium-sized dining room.

"What do you think," Barry asked her.

"I love it," Tracy replied seriously.

"When do want to close, Tracy?" Barry asked.

"I think I can close in two or three weeks," Tracy said, making plans to use her nest egg.

"You're saying I have a cash deal?"

"Of course, Barry, unless you want to wait three months for the sale."

"No, no," Barry said. "This calls for a celebration, and I'm taking care of everything."

Tracy laughed. Barry never missed an opportunity to take her out if she allowed him to. She thought that Barry was in his late forties, but it was hard to guess his age. Barry was one of those people who grew old gracefully. Added to that, he was so much fun, especially when the agents attended-out-of town conferences.

"Are we going dancing, Barry?" Tracy laughed again, knowing how much Barry loved dancing. However, she wasn't in a dancing mood tonight.

"Would you like to go to Hannah's for dinner?"

"No," Tracy said. She spent enough time at Hannah's. And if she did dine at her sister's restaurant, she ran the risk of seeing Evan.

"Think of a place to go, Tracy," Barry said. He opened the door and waited for her to walk out into the corridor as he locked the door to the apartment.

"I'll tell you what. . . ." Tracy bargained.

"What?" Barry twisted the key in the lock, and they walked to the elevator.

"After I move and get settled, we'll go out."

"Just name the place and the time, Tracy, and I'll be there," he assured her.

Tracy was glad that he agreed with her. She didn't feel like going out for the evening. Nothing she did would be a simple solution to the mess she'd made, allowing Evan to love her, arousing feelings that she thought had died along with Drake. "I'll call you," she said, wanting to go home and comfort her wounded heart.

"Are you sure you're all right?" Barry pried.

"I'm okay." She told him a half-truth. In a

way she was fine. She'd managed to find the perfect condo, and Barry would take care of the transaction. However, she was also aware that Barry liked her, and it wasn't because she was an agent. He'd wanted to take her out only months after Drake's death. She'd refused, knowing that he would think that she was interested in a relationship. They eventually discussed the issue, and his desire to date her seemed to dissolve. Tonight, she knew that he was as excited as any real estate agent would be to have a buyer paying cash for property.

"I'll be waiting for your call," Barry said as they took the elevator to the lobby.

That night, Tracy didn't sleep well. She tossed and turned until early the next morning, worrying, and wondering why Evan chose not to be honest with her. Why had he conned her into thinking that he was interested in a relationship, when he knew all along that he wanted something different? Finally, she surrendered to exhaustion and slept without dreaming. She woke tired and red-eyed.

Regardless of her fatigue, Tracy started her day by packing. Even though it would be a few weeks before she actually moved, staying busy helped to free her mind from unwanted thoughts. She planned to leave the furniture and take only her clothes and other personal belongings. When she finished packing, she bought a FOR SALE sign for Drake's truck and called her nephew, Shun, to wash and wax it.

Tracy sat on her patio, among her beautiful flowers, sipping a tall glass of cool spring water.

Without warning, her mind brought up uncontrolled memories of Evan. He had been special to her. She'd allowed herself to withdraw from the cocoon she'd buried her emotions in and stroll graciously down the primrose path filled with passion, only to find spurs and debris on the trail.

Tracy dismissed the awful musing and called Hannah.

"Hannah's—"

"Hannah," Tracy said, not giving her sister time to finish.

"Tracy, I'm surprised to hear from you on a Sunday."

"Do you need me tonight?"

"Of course. Come over." She could almost hear the smile in her sister's voice. "Shun is having a fit because he wants to go out with his friends tonight. I'm sure he would appreciate it if you host for him."

"I'm on my way," Tracy said. She hung up and went upstairs to shower and put on the black dress that was the uniform for Hannah's dinner club.

As she dressed, she brushed away one thought after another that clicked through her mind concerning Evan. She was going to Hannah's to work, hoping to be too absorbed in her duties to think about him.

She would be safe at Hannah's. She could camouflage her inner battle, and for a few hours she would find peace.

Twelve

"I found this beautiful condo for sale," Tracy told Hannah as they sat in Hannah's office waiting to relieve Shun. After she spoke, she noticed the happiness in Hannah's eyes.

"I guess it's for the best that you sell the house," she said. "Maybe now you can start living again."

Tracy looked away from her sister, struggling to push away the mistake she had made, thinking that she'd found a new life filled with love and respect. At that moment, she was glad she had not introduced Evan to the family.

"I think it's about time that I moved on," Tracy replied, checking her watch and preparing to relieve her nephew. "We'll talk later," she said. "I can imagine Shun is wondering what happened to me."

"Oh, I tried to call you back, but you'd already left," Hannah said to Tracy. "Shun and his friends changed their plans, but if you want to help out here, be my guest."

"I have an idea," Tracy suggested to Hannah. It seemed that her sister and brother-in-law spent their entire lives working. The only fun they ever had was a fishing or camping trip once or twice a year.

Hannah raised an eyebrow. "You do?"

"You and Jordan can go home, and Shun and I will take care of things here."

"Are you serious?" Hannah sounded surprised.

"I don't tease about work or fun." Tracy smiled, getting up and taking Hannah's purse from the closet. "Go." She pushed her toward the door.

"All right, I'm going—but first let me show you the payroll and this information." Hannah pulled out a file. "This newest employee needs to fill out his W-2 form." Hannah placed the folder in front of Tracy. "Make sure he completes this form tonight."

"I will," Tracy agreed, opening the folder to study the form.

"And the young lady in the expediting room always gets help from the waiters at the end of the evening," Hannah said, pointing at the room. "Make sure those guys help her."

"How am I going to get the waiters to stay and help?"

"Well, that's the new rule."

"When did you make that rule?"

"A few weeks ago. The expediter makes all the coffee and soft drinks, and she makes sure the waiters get what they need to speed up service. The waiters go back there while they're waiting for their tables—and eat, scatter glasses, drink up the cappuccino—you name it, they'll do it. The place is a mess by the end of the evening." Hannah waved her long, delicate fingers. "The least they can do is help her stack the dishes and glasses for the dishwasher."

"I understand, and I'll deal with it." Tracy gave Hannah a playful push. "You and Jordan go out and have fun."

"Thank you, Tracy. You're a doll."

"I know, and you're welcome," Tracy teased, laughing.

Once Hannah was gone, Tracy settled down to work. Hannah and Jordan had been good to her for so many years. When their mother died, Hannah was in her first year of college, and Jordan was in his junior year. Hannah withdrew from college to raise her. Tracy learned that after she was much older, Hannah asked Jordan to marry her. That way, Tracy wouldn't have to live with their aunt. Their father's sister, Ada, asked to raised Tracy when their mother died. But Hannah wouldn't hear of it. Since she and Jordan had planned to get married once they graduated college she decided to ask Jordan if he would he marry her sooner. She explained that she wanted to keep Tracy with her, and Jordan agreed to marry her.

Hannah knew how old-fashioned her aunt was. Her aunt Ada thought if a woman was responsible enough to have a husband then she would have no problem taking care of a child. In her aunt's mind the age of the child didn't matter.

Hannah took a job, working full-time in the restaurant that now bore her name, while Jordan worked part-time with her on the weekends.

Jordan graduated with a major in business administration and a minor in hotel and restaurant management.

Shortly afterward, the owner hired Jordan to manage the establishment. When he retired, he offered Hannah and Jordan the first chance at buying the restaurant. They got a loan from the bank and purchased the business. They turned the restaurant into a dinner club and named it "Hannah's."

Tracy went to school and did her homework during the week. She worked in the restaurant on the weekends and a few hours each week. Every Saturday night, she went skating. She met Regina at the skating rink, and they became best friends. Regina and Tracy enjoyed each other's company so much that she begged Hannah and Jordan to hire Regina to work at the restaurant. Reluctantly, they hired Regina—with a warning to both girls: If Tracy and Regina spent more time socializing than working, Regina would be terminated.

All through high school, Tracy and Regina worked at Hannah's, until they left for college. On holidays—especially Christmas and spring break—they once again took their rightful places at Hannah's and worked short hours before going out with their respective boyfriends.

Tracy had paid her dues at Hannah's. Her first job was as the dishwasher. She was later promoted to hostess. When Tracy was in her senior year in college, Jordan taught her the art of mixing drinks.

During her last year of college, Tracy met

Drake in the dinner club—and everything in her life was history. A month after graduation, she and Drake were married.

"Tracy!" Shun burst into the office. "A guy is out there looking for you."

Tracy looked at Shun. He was tall, with coffee-cream brown skin, a head of huge, black curls, and long, thick lashes that any woman would wrestle him for.

"Who is it, Shun?" Tracy looked back at the account she was working on.

"I don't know. He didn't tell me his name."

Tracy hoped that Evan hadn't lost his mind and had come looking for her again. "Describe him."

"Tracy, he's a guy, okay." Shun stretched his wide hands, which looked like they belonged to an NFL player.

"Is he tall or short? What's his eye color?" Tracy asked, thinking that Shun would've noticed Evan's charcoal-gray eyes.

"Look, I wasn't sizing the guy up and looking into his eyes. . . . What do you want from me?"

"Boy, you don't pay attention to anything."

"Sorry, Tracy, but I save my admiration for the women."

"Child, please," she said, thinking that maybe it was Barry who had tracked her down. She carefully marked what she was working on with a self-adhesive flag and walked out to the bar area.

She moved closer and looked out into the club, scanning the bar area and the diners. She didn't know who was around the L-shaped corner, hiding in the shadow of the tall palms, which Hannah had recently bought for the summer months.

There was no one at the bar except the regulars and a few strange faces. Other than that, Tracy saw no one that could have asked for her. She inched closer to the edge of the bar, hoping to get a better view.

"Tracy, we have to talk."

She wheeled around to the familiar-sounding voice. Evan stood next to one of Hannah's new trees. His black suit, black shirt, and black tie made him look even more handsome than she remembered.

"I'm busy," Tracy said, turning to go to the office. Evan reached across the counter and grabbed her wrist.

"Let go of me," she said, pulling against his firm grip.

"I need to explain everything to you." Evan's voice was low and unrelenting.

"We have nothing to discuss," Tracy stated, trying to loosen the grip he had on her hand without the clients at the bar noticing her struggle.

"I'm not letting you go until I talk to you."

She had work pending in Hannah's office, and she'd promised her sister that she would take care of it. "We'll talk after work." She couldn't possibly stand there all night while Evan refused to let her get back to work.

"What time do you leave?" he asked.

"It's going to be late, Evan," Tracy said, hoping that he would leave, or at least leave her to her work and give up waiting for her.

"I'll wait for you," he said, releasing her wrist.

"Don't wait for me." She turned and went to the office. For the remainder of the evening, she struggled to keep any thoughts of Evan from occupying her mind. But freeing her mind of Evan was a task within itself. Visions of Evan's actions played in her mind—his touch, the tender, yet firm way he held her wrist, the direct way he looked at her. His gaze seemed to drill through the ice that surrounded her heart. She wanted to run to him and kiss him, to feel his soft beard brush gently against her cheek. But she couldn't do any of those things with Evan. He'd betrayed her emotions, her heart, and her trust, and now he wanted to clarify his actions.

The evening finally ended. The waiters and the expediter got into an argument over job descriptions and were on the verge of fighting when Tracy reached the crowded expediting room. The chef had pitched a pot lid through the expediting window, scattering the crowd and breaking up the verbal fight. It didn't matter to him that he almost struck a waiter, reminding Tracy to speak to Hannah regarding Chef Marvin's temper and dangerous actions. Maybe, if Hannah spoke to Marvin, he would calm down. Tracy was sure if the chef continued pitching pot lids, aiming them at the employees, one of the workers would be struck and Hannah and Jordan would find themselves involved in a lawsuit.

Tracy vowed that she would never offer to

work in Hannah's office again. She would work the bar, or work as the hostess for a night or two, and when her services weren't needed, she would find a book to read in the comfort of her home.

As the employees left the restaurant, Tracy, Shun, and the chef made sure that the restaurant was locked and the security system was armed before going to their cars.

As she walked across the well-lit parking lot, Tracy noticed a tall, masculine figure leaning against her car. She knew it was Evan.

"Who's standing beside your car?" the chef asked Tracy.

"A friend," she answered, noticing that Evan had folded his arms across his chest.

"Do you want us to wait for you, Tracy?" Shun asked, sensing her discomfort.

"Yes, wait for me," she said, walking to the car and preparing to unlock the door, get in, and go home.

"Evan we can talk another time. It's late, and I have to get home," Tracy, said.

He towered over her, his lips close to hers. She felt his hot, fresh breath against her face. "We have to talk *now*. My place or yours, it doesn't matter."

Tracy knew that she wasn't getting rid of him tonight. "Only for a few minutes, at your place." She unlocked her car door.

"I'm driving," Evan said.

"No, I'll give you a ride."

"Are you all right, Tracy?" Shun asked.

"I'm okay," she acknowledged her nephew's concern for her safety.

"Who're those guys?" Evan asked, referring to Shun and the chef.

"Shun?" Tracy called out to her nephew.

"Yes, Tracy."

"This is Evan Maxwell, and Evan"—she looked at the man who was impossible to forget—"this is Shun, my nephew."

"What's up, man?" Shun extended his hand to Evan.

"I'm good," Evan replied, meeting Shun's grip.

Tracy introduced Evan to the chef just as he was about to drive out of the lot.

"Good night, Shun." Tracy waved to him. "Drive careful."

"Where's your car?" Tracy turned to Evan and asked, almost forgetting that she was angry at him.

"I went to the island. And, of course, I've been back in Atlanta for only a few hours. I need to rent another car." He walked around and waited for her to unlock the door for him.

"Are you living in the same hotel?" she inquired, getting in and turning the key in the ignition.

"Yes," Evan said.

"Tracy . . ."

"I don't want to talk, Evan, unless you have an explanation for that phone conversation I overheard."

"I can explain."

Tracy took her eyes off the street and looked at him quickly. "Well?"

"Can it wait until we're in my room?"

Tracy knew that she should have demanded for Evan to tell her about the call while they were on their way to his hotel. But tonight, she would be strong. She would listen, and then she would leave him in his hotel room. She understood clearly that things weren't that simple when she was alone with Evan. While she drove him to his hotel, she stayed quiet and gathered her strength. They rode to his hotel in silence. Tracy stole glances at Evan. He was too quiet and appeared to be deep in thought.

Tracy sped up, passing lanky buildings that resembled stacked blocks with tiny bands of light flaring out from small cracks. She stole another glance at Evan. She wasn't sure what was going on with him or what he was thinking. But she had an idea that she might not like what was going through his mind. She slowed and stopped at a light, noticing that Evan was resting his head against the leather seat. He maintained that position until she found a space in the hotel parking lot.

"I don't think I should go inside," she said, forcing herself not to look at him. If she did, she might lose her resolve and find herself forgiving him before he even explained.

"Come inside with me, Tracy," Evan said. "I don't want any distractions."

She agreed silently and got out of the car. Tracy hoped she wasn't making a mistake. Once inside his suite, she sat on the sofa's arm. "I'm listening," she said, determined to keep her emotions from surfacing.

Evan rubbed the back of his neck as if unsure about where to begin. "You visited St. Hope Isle."

Tracy glanced at him quickly, then lowered her gaze. She could still feel his eyes burning into her. "Yes, I was there for a few days."

"You bought a bag with several pieces of fake jewelry."

She looked at him then. "Yes."

Evan ran his finger over his mustache, then continued. "There's a diamond necklace inside the bag."

"A what?" Tracy could hardly believe what he was saying to her. Besides, she had taken the bag to Janet for the women to use at the WINOH program.

"The necklace belongs to an ex-friend, and he wants me to bring it back to him."

Tracy waited for Evan to continue. When he didn't, she spoke up. "Evan, I bought a bag of fake jewelry from a woman at a yard sale. Are you telling me that the woman is an old friend of yours?"

"No. She's not a friend. Wilma was with my father for years. She was closing the house and selling everything."

"So, who owns the jewelry?" Tracy was suspicious.

"The fake jewelry probably belonged to Wilma, but Frank Johnson owns the necklace," Evan said.

"And Frank Johnson is your friend?" Tracy asked.

"I use to hang around with him when we were kids."

Frank Johnson. Tracy remembered the name and the man. She was right, he had followed her until she disappeared into the crowd. He was also at the party the same evening. "Evan I don't know what's going on, but I will get the necklace back to you because this jewelry business scares me."

"I'm sorry that I didn't talk to you about the necklace earlier, Tracy."

"You could have asked me. I would have given the necklace to you." Her fears began to rise, escalating another notch. She didn't know if the necklace was still in the bag. The jewelry could have been with any of the women who attended the center.

Which meant . . . she didn't want to think what might happen to her if she couldn't find the necklace. "What does Frank plan to do if you don't return the necklace?" Tracy asked.

"He threatened to destroy my businesses," Evan replied.

Tracy realized Frank was dangerous. "I don't want anything to happen to me," Tracy said, hoping she would find out who had the expensive necklace so she could return it to Evan as quickly as possible. "I'll call you when I get this piece of jewelry, and after that, I don't want to see you again."

"Tracy I'm not going to let Frank hurt you." She watched him move toward her. She was frozen on the edge of the sofa's arm, anticipating his close contact.

"Tracy, you're the best woman friend I've ever had. I love you, but I want us to always remain friends." He touched her shoulder.

"I don't expect you to say anything different." She stood, moving away from his touch.

"I'm sorry," Evan apologized. "I'll do whatever I can to make things right with us again." He put his arms around her waist, and held her at arm's length.

"I'll get the jewelry for you, Evan," Tracy said, forcing herself not to look at him while untangling herself from his grasp. "Good night." She walked to the door, opened it, and walked out into the corridor.

"Tracy, don't leave." Evan was beside her, his quick pace matching her steps.

"I'll call you when I have the necklace," she responded, steadying the tremble in her voice as she hurried to the elevator with tears burning her eyes. She blinked and allowed the tears to roll freely. It was her fault. She was a love-starved widow who had allowed herself to fall in love with a man she didn't know.

It is going to take weeks to get over him, Tracy mused as she stepped off the elevator and walked through the lobby. If she weren't careful, she was going to find herself in a therapist's office, learning ways to avoid men as good-looking and charming as Evan Maxwell.

Thirteen

A week later, Tracy felt excitement radiating through her as she entered the Women in Need of Help building. Evan's company had shipped the donated computers, as promised.

"This is great," Janet said, marveling over the program's success. "Tracy, I believe the program is going to survive."

"I never doubted the program would succeed," Tracy expressed with a cheerful, optimistic attitude.

It was encouraging to know that Evan kept his word regarding the computers. Still, her heart felt weighted with steel. She'd considered him her lover until she had discovered his reasons for pursuing her.

"I didn't think the program would fail, either," Janet said. "But it's great to see so many people helping us." She sank into the chair behind her desk and let out a sigh. "It's wonderful."

"Yes, it is," Tracy replied, hoping that Janet still had the jewelry safely tucked away in the file cabinet. The sooner she returned the diamond necklace to Evan, the sooner she would be free of him. "Janet, do you have the jewelry?"

"I have a few pieces," Janet said. "I gave most of it away."

"Can I see it?" Tracy asked.

"Sure." Janet rose and went to the file cabinet. "You aren't thinking of taking them back, are you?"

"No," Tracy replied, realizing she'd answered too quickly. But she couldn't tell Janet that there was an authentic diamond necklace among the fake accessories.

"Good." Janet opened the file drawer and took out the brown bag. "Because Linda was thrilled with the necklace she wore for her interview."

"Necklace?" Tracy asked.

"Yes." Janet chuckled. "I told Linda that if she wore that fake diamond, the boss might think she didn't need the job."

Tracy's spirits sank. She didn't bother opening the bag and gave it back to Janet. "Janet, the owner wants the necklace back. I promised I would return it," Tracy said, not disclosing any of the details.

"Well, Miss Linda told me she was going out of town." Janet took the bag of jewelry and put it in the drawer. "She's visiting her sister and some friends in Augusta." Janet locked the file cabinet and returned to her desk.

"I hate to disappoint her, but I need the necklace." Tracy responded. "Was she planning on leaving tonight?"

"I'm not sure. I'll give her a call." Janet dialed

Linda's home number. Within seconds, she was speaking to someone.

From the conversation, Tracy realized that Linda had already left. She felt her heart sink. If Linda misplaced the necklace, or if the necklace was stolen, Tracy wasn't sure what would happen to her. It was almost amusing how a simple trip to an island could create so much trouble.

Janet hung up. "Linda is on her way to Augusta as we speak."

"I should've asked you to get her sister's address," Tracy said, not losing hope.

"I already have the address," Janet replied, flipping through her Rolodex. "Yes, here it is," she said, writing the address on an index card while simultaneously explaining to Tracy how Linda's sister had been in the program years ago. "When she got a job in Augusta and moved, she gave me her address." Janet gave the address to Tracy.

"Thanks, Janet," Tracy said, placing the address in her purse. She planned to call Linda as soon as she got home. But first she wanted to see the computers Evan had donated to the program.

"I think I'll go up and take a look at the computers." Tracy headed toward the door.

"I'll go with you," Janet offered, getting up from her desk. "Sometimes I can hardly believe Mr. Maxwell was so generous."

He's even more generous with his affection, Tracy thought. Janet was not aware of the tryst she and Evan had shared, and Tracy wasn't divulging any information.

Together, they walked to the classroom. There were four long tables in rows on each side of the room, and four new computers sat on each table. Business and clerical book lined bookshelves built into the wall. Several posters displaying students engaged in study hung on the walls.

As Tracy viewed the equipment, disquieting thoughts tangled in her mind like spider webs. Evan was charitable—except with the knowledge he'd kept from her regarding the necklace. She would have to live with her disappointment.

"I have to personally thank Mr. Maxwell," Janet said, still marveling over the computers.

Tracy was quiet. The less said about Evan the better. However, she could blame Evan for only half of the problem, realizing that she blamed herself, also. She had been thrilled by his touch, his affection, and his charisma, allowing feelings that she thought she would never know again to be aroused.

"Well, Tracy, what do you think?"

"I was surprised when he offered to donate the computers," Tracy said, leaving the conversation at that. *If Janet only knew what I've been thinking, she would be surprised,* Tracy mused. She hadn't told Janet about Evan. Neither had she told Hannah or Betty. She had wanted to keep it private, just in case things didn't work out between them. She was glad now to have followed her instincts because after she returned the necklace to him, she wouldn't see him anymore.

Tracy and Janet left the room after they'd discussed the details of the instructors Janet knew were volunteering. "I'll see you later," Tracy said to Janet as she left the classroom, and she was on her way out the building.

With the Atlanta thief still free, Tracy walked to her car quickly. She heard footsteps close behind her. Tracy hurried to her car. As the footsteps quickened behind her, Tracy's apprehension escalated.

Tracy thought she heard someone calling her name, but she didn't dare look back. Even though she was sure a burglar wouldn't know her name, she sped up.

"Wait!" She heard a masculine voice call out to her again.

She began to trot faster toward her car now. Suddenly she tripped over a small tin container in her path and fell. She dropped her purse, the contents scattering onto the pavement. Tracy winced at the pain racing through her ankle.

"Oh, my God, let me help you." Evan straddled her, his muscular thighs resting against her hips.

Tracy turned and faced him. The pain in her ankle was almost too much to bear.

"Are you hurt?" he asked, gathering her in his arms and attempting to lift her to her feet.

"Ouch!" Her face contorted with pain. "It's my ankle."

"I'm sorry I frightened you." Evan crouched

over her. "Come here." He made a second attempt to draw her up to him.

"Why are you here?" she asked.

"I stopped by to make sure the computers had arrived. I saw you and. . . ." His voice trailed off. "Maybe I should take you to the hospital."

Tracy turned her face away from Evan. "I'm fine. If my ankle is still hurting in the morning, I'll see a doctor." She struggled against him, trying to sit up and remove herself from his embrace.

"Tracy, we need to make sure you're all right." Evan demanded.

Tracy stood, bracing herself against his body. "Ouch," she groaned, lifting her foot to avoid putting any more pressure on her throbbing ankle.

"Where is your car key?" Evan asked.

"I have it," Tracy answered, still holding the key in her hand.

"Give it to me."

"I can drive myself home," Tracy said, not wanting any special treatment from Evan. Just being in his presence was almost spellbinding. If she allowed him to drive her home, he might think things were right between them. She simply lost all of her good sense when she was with Evan.

"I'm driving you to the emergency room," Evan remarked, assisting her to the passenger side of her car, "as soon as I pick up all this stuff that fell out of your purse."

When Tracy was seated inside the car, Evan

squatted and stroked her ankle gently, feeling for broken bones.

"Don't do that, it hurts," Tracy said, not wanting to be helpless and have Evan as her caretaker.

"It doesn't feel as if it's broken." He rose and picked up the contents of her purse.

Tracy fought her inner battle. The more she resisted Evan, the more a compelling fate forced them together.

Tracy had finally removed her wedding photograph from the mantel and had packed it away. She thought that she had packed away all of her mixed emotions concerning Evan, too. But tonight was proof that her emotions remained intact. With all of her mixed affections, she still knew that she cared about Evan, regardless of what she told herself. Evan was nice, sensitive, kind, and generous, but deep in the recesses of her mind, she felt that there was more to him than the smooth, easygoing, sentimental person that he that he appeared to be.

Evan slid in beside her and set her purse between them. Without speaking, he drove to the hospital.

"Are you sure you put everything in my purse?" Tracy asked, breaking the silence.

"I think I got everything," he said, glancing over at her.

"My phone." Tracy reached inside her purse and searched, pulling out the cellular. "Let's just hope it's not broken," she said, punching a button and watching yellow light illuminate the miniature window.

"If it's broken, I'll replace it," Evan promised, reaching over and touching her hand with his fingers.

"That won't be necessary," Tracy said, as the phone let out a musical beep. Even if the phone was broken she wouldn't allow him to buy a new one or pay for repairs.

"I know you're upset, Tracy. But we had a misunderstanding," Evan said, not taking his eyes off the street. "If I would've told you about the necklace when I met you . . ."

"What are you saying, Evan?" Tracy said, after noticing Evan's pause.

"I don't know if we would've gotten to know each other," he said.

"It would've saved us a lot of trouble."

"Maybe."

Tracy didn't respond to him. With an aching ankle, she was not in the mood to discuss the diamond necklace. But since he broached the subject, she thought this was a good time to tell him that she knew who had the jewelry. And she was prepared to give him the diamond as soon as she paid a visit to Linda.

"I'll be returning the necklace to you soon," Tracy said as Evan drove to the emergency room entrance and stopped.

"Good, the sooner I get the necklace to the owner, the happier I'll be." Evan got out. "I'll be right back. I'm going to get you a wheelchair."

"I don't need a wheelchair," Tracy countered. But Evan was already halfway to the hospital door.

She wasn't exactly amazed at the attention Evan was giving her. However, his attentiveness made her even more aware that there was something special about him. But she imagined that he was like most people in the world. Everyone had a good side. It was Evan's bad side that worried her. And she didn't know if he really was as bad as she thought he was.

Minutes later, Evan returned with a nurse dressed in orange scrubs, rolling a wheelchair out to the car. Tracy waited patiently while Evan opened the door for her and helped her with the nurse's assistance to the chair.

The hospital's glass door slid open, and the nurse wheeled Tracy into the cool, well-lit emergency room.

"Wait here, Mr. Maxwell," the nurse said as she wheeled Tracy into a room.

With the assistance of another nurse, Tracy was helped onto a narrow examination bed. After much probing and X rays, Tracy learned from her doctor that her ankle was twisted. After the ankle had been wrapped with a bandage, Tracy was given a small package of pain medication, with instructions to stay off the ankle for the remainder of the evening.

"Are you all right, Tracy?" Evan rose from the chair he'd been sitting in and went over to her as soon as the nurse rolled her out of the examination room and into the waiting area.

"I'm fine. I have a twisted ankle."

"She's fine, Mr. Maxwell. But you'll have to help her out tonight. The less pressure she puts on her ankle, the quicker it will heal," the nurse suggested to Evan as she wheeled Tracy back to the car.

Soon, Evan was driving her to his hotel. Tracy had planned to go to Augusta the following day to get the necklace from Linda. Thanks to Evan, she probably wouldn't be able to do that. If she felt better by morning, however, she was going to make the trip.

"Evan, did it occur to you that I might want to go home?" Tracy inquired.

"Tracy, I realize that you want to go home. But I need to make sure you're all right tonight. You heard the nurse."

She had heard the nurse, but the nurse didn't understand that she and Evan had issues. "Let's get your car, and I'll drive myself home from there," Tracy said. She didn't want to be close to Evan anymore. Sleeping at his hotel would distract her, and the promises she'd made not to involve herself with him again would be broken. She needed space and time to collect her thoughts, and maybe in the future they could be casual friends.

"If that's what you want," Evan said. "But, I'm driving you home. I'll get my car tomorrow." Tracy thought she detected a twinge of disappointment in his voice.

"No, Evan, I'll be fine," she told him as he drove to the WINOH center to get his car.

When they arrived, Tracy got out with Evan's assistance and allowed him to help her to the driver's side of her car.

"I'm following you home," Evan said, closing her car door and going to his car.

As she drove home, she was thankful that it was her left ankle that was slightly injured. Otherwise, she wouldn't be able to drive.

She was soon thinking about the evening's events. Even in her fear, she had been full with joy at seeing him. But she was still not changing her plans to discontinue their friendship.

She pulled into her driveway and raised the garage door. She drove in and cut the engine and the lights. Tracy noticed in her rearview mirror that Evan was out of his car and walking up the driveway.

"Let me help you," he said as she eased out of the car, trying to put only a minimum amount of weight on her ankle.

She accepted his support without defiance. She allowed herself to be half-carried and half-walked into her kitchen. Tracy flipped the light switch. "I'm sleeping in the study," she said, allowing him to help her get seated on the sofa.

"Do you need anything?" Evan asked her.

"If you don't mind, I would like my gown and housecoat, bedroom shoes, and bath things from the bedroom upstairs." Tracy was glad that Evan insisted on seeing her home now. She knew that Hannah wouldn't mind helping, but Evan was with her and already willing to help. "My bedroom is the first door on the left," she said, wincing at the pain shooting through her ankle.

Soon Evan returned carrying a long, black silk gown, which was not exactly what Tracy had in mind. But it had to serve the purpose since she was in no condition to go up and get her comfortable, long, white, cotton gown.

"Thanks, Evan," Tracy said, as he carefully set her black bedroom slippers down in front of her, then gave her the basket that held her soap and other toiletries.

"Do you need any help getting out of your clothes?" Evan asked.

"No. If you'll excuse me, I can manage." She waited for him to leave the room before she slipped out of her dress. Tracy took the comb from the basket and began to comb and braid her hair. Since her ankle wasn't sprained or broken, she unwrapped the bandage. She couldn't go to bed without first taking a shower. Tracy lay the bandage beside her on the sofa and noticed a slight swelling, "Evan?" Tracy called to him.

"What do you need, Tracy?"

"There's a cane in the coat closet near the front door. Will you bring it to me?"

"Why did you unwrap your ankle?"

"I need to take a shower, and I don't want the bandage to get wet."

"It would be easier if I help you take your shower."

"Evan."

"All right, Tracy." He left the room.

In less than a minute, he returned. "Let me help you."

"I can manage, thank you." Tracy took her gown and towel. Steadying herself with the support of the cane, she walked to the study's bath, leaving Evan in the room.

Carefully, she discarded her clothes and showered. Tracy was sure she'd taken the quickest shower in history, but she had to wash the sticky heat and grime from the day off her.

When she returned to the room, Evan brought in a sheet and pillow. "I took these from the linen closet," he said, spreading the sheet and laying the pillow on the sofa.

"Thanks, Evan." Tracy eased down on the sofa and began rewrapping her ankle when Evan took the bandage from her.

"Let me do this," he said, kneeling before her. Like an expert, he arranged the gauze around her ankle. "Is it too tight?"

"It's okay."

He hooked the small silver clamp and sat back on his heels while she settled on the sofa.

"Are you sure you don't want me to stay with you tonight?"

"I think I'll be fine." Tracy smiled at him. "If I'm feeling better tomorrow afternoon, I'm going to Augusta to get the necklace." Tracy rose and looked at Evan, who was still sitting on his heels in front of her.

"I'm going with you," he stated.

"It's not necessary for you to come with me." She was careful to maintain her composure because having him near her was already causing problems for her libido.

Evan stood and leaned down, kissing her. "I'll see you tomorrow."

She watched as he left the study. "Lock the door on your way out."

The only sound she heard was the soft click

of the front door closing behind him. She closed her eyes and tried to sleep. How attentive Evan had been to her was almost enough to make her forgive him. She licked her lips, still feeling his kiss. She finally dozed off, catching wisps of sleep in between wanting Evan and wanting the pain in her ankle to go away. Regardless of how attentive he had been to her, she was not getting tangled up in his web.

Fourteen

The next day, Evan met with his new staff. After the meeting, he headed over to his mother's house. He had slept at her house last night. His mother lived a few blocks away from Tracy. He hadn't felt like driving into the city; and just in case Tracy needed him, he would only have a few blocks to travel.

Mavis Maxwell was already in bed when he arrived last night. She asked him to visit with her the next day, if he could find the time. To Evan, finding time to visit with his mother was not a problem, although he admitted that he had been busy and hadn't stopped by to visit her while he was in Atlanta as often as he could have.

He had valid reasons. First, he hadn't planned to get to know Tracy after he met her. To his surprise, he had fallen in love with her and spent most of his time either loving her, wanting to be with her, or fighting with her.

As he went to his mother's house, Evan recalled last night's events. He'd sat in his car in front of Tracy's house for a long time before he went to his mother's home. He wasn't sure

how he was going to change Tracy's mind about
him. He figured that he had bitten off more
than he could chew. She was still in love with
her husband. He didn't have to be trampled by
a herd of wild horses to understand that issue.
He assumed that the red truck in the yard had
belonged to her husband. Even though the wedding pictures were no longer displayed on the
mantel, she still hadn't taken her husband's certificates and awards off the wall in the study. He
had competed with a few good men for the affection of the women he wanted in his day, but
he'd never competed with a dead man. Evan
wasn't sure how he was going to solve the problem, but he knew he couldn't give up. He
wanted Tracy, and he intended to show her just
how much he wanted her. He cut his engine,
took long strides to his mother's front door, and
rang the bell.

Mavis Maxwell opened the door for her twin
son. "Well. You found time to come by and visit
with me," she said, going to the living room.

"You know I always have time for you." Evan
followed her into the living room, sat on the
gray wingback chair, and stretched his long legs.
His mother seemed to never change. She grew
old gracefully. To Evan she appeared much like
she did to him when he was a boy.

A silver strand waved the top of her black
hair. Her cappuccino skin was smooth and free
of wrinkles. Her hands were well manicured and
appeared soft. One year away from sixty—and
his mother could've passed for a younger age.

Mavis reached over and took a letter out of

a wicker basket on the end table. "This came in the mail yesterday," she said, getting up and handing the letter to Evan. "Read it."

Evan couldn't imagine why she wanted him to read her mail. But he slipped the letter out of the envelope and read it. When he finished, he gave the letter to his mother.

"The house. . . ." Evan started. "I thought daddy remarried." Evan was as shocked as his mother to learn that his father had never married the woman who he had taken Evan and Keith to live with before he shipped them off to England. "He left the house and the business to you."

"It seems that way. I have no idea what to do with an import/export business," Mavis said to her son.

"Does Keith know about this?" Evan asked. Their father had never spoken about their mother to either of them as far as Evan could recall. At the mere mention of Mavis' name, he would seem angry. So, why would he bequeath their mother his company and home?

"No, I thought I would speak to you first, since you live on the island." Mavis stood and walked over to the wide window, gracefully tugging at her long top, which matched her green, knee-length shorts.

"I don't want any trouble with lawyers and the court." She placed her hands on her hips. "I thought your father married that . . . siren woman."

"I thought he married her too." Evan replied.

"But Evan, what am I supposed to do with this?"

"You don't want it?"

"I don't know. I'm not up for a good fight these days." She smiled. "Especially if the woman who we all thought was Baily's wife decides to protest."

"Are you all right?" Evan asked.

"Of course, I'm fine. It's just that Baily always found a way to get on my nerves."

Evan never could figure out why his parents divorced, and at this moment he wasn't even sure if they *were* divorced. "You and daddy got a divorce, right?"

Mavis turned to her son. "Yes."

"I'll get Keith, and we'll look into it. In the meantime, you need to stop worrying. Relationships!" Evan said under his breath and got up to leave.

"What about relationships?" Mavis asked.

"Nothing. I was just thinking out loud."

"Which reminds me, Evan, are you ever going to marry and start a family?"

He stopped walking, and without turning to look at his mother, he spoke loud enough for her to hear. "First, I'll have to find someone to marry me. At the rate things are going now, I doubt I ever will," he said, waiting for his mother's response.

Mavis chuckled. "Evan, you need to settle down."

"I'm working on it."

"Really? When do I get to meet her?"

"I'll see you later, Mother." Evan said without

answering her question. He doubted that Tracy had ever considered marriage to anyone except Drake Wilson. Evan felt a streak of jealousy course through him. "We'll talk soon," Evan promised his mother. He figured that she wouldn't be satisfied until he and Keith made sure that no one would be forcing her to go to court. He noticed that his mother seemed to have mellowed over the years.

As he drove to Tracy's house, Evan remembered how their aunt had once refused to let him and Keith visit their mother one Christmas because their father had ordered their aunt not to allow them to visit. Their mother hadn't tolerated their father's actions. No one kept her from seeing her children. She boarded a plane to England and visited them. When she thought they were out of hearing distance, Mavis Maxwell used words that any self-respecting pirate would've been proud of.

Evan parked at the curb nearest to Tracy's house and walked to her door. A few minutes later, she let him inside. Tracy was dressed in a pair of blue shorts and a white top, and she was wearing a pair of white tennis shoes. She looked as if she were about to leave.

"How's the ankle?" he asked, noticing that she had removed the bandage.

"It feels much better. I think I'll be all right," Tracy said.

"So, you *do* feel up to taking that ride to Augusta."

"I am going to Augusta. Alone."

"I told you last night, Tracy. *We* are going to

Augusta. You're in no condition to take the trip alone."

"If I need your assistance, I will ask for it." He didn't like the tone of Tracy's voice; she sounded upset with him. But whether she liked it or not, he was going with her to Augusta, Georgia.

"Are you leaving now?" Evan asked.

"Those were my intentions."

"Then we better get out of here." Without thinking, Evan stood behind Tracy and slipped his arms around her waist while she locked the door. When she finished and turned to him, he forgot that she was still in love with her deceased husband and he kissed her. "Tracy," he smothered her name across her lips.

Fifteen

By the time Tracy and Evan arrived at Linda's sister's house, it was already dusk. Several young girls were sitting on the lighted front porch. Some were playing with dolls, while others molded objects from multicolored clay. An older woman sat in a faded, wooden rocking chair, braiding a young girl's hair. The woman's yellow skin and gray hair was ashen against the early evening dusk.

Evan got out and walked to the porch. He spoke to a woman who appeared to be the children's grandmother. "Hello. I'm here to see a young lady." He looked back to the car at Tracy. "My friend in the car said the woman's name is Linda."

The woman stopped braiding the girl's hair. "Is Linda in trouble?" From where Tracy sat waiting for Evan, she could detect worry and concern in the woman's voice.

"No, I just need to talk to her." Tracy heard Evan say.

"She and her sister went to the park," the woman said and began braiding another pigtail into the small girl's hair.

"Which park did she go to?"

Tracy prayed that Linda was not wearing the necklace. She couldn't stand sitting in the car any longer, listening to the conversation through the open window. Her ankle was slightly sore, but she could walk, even if her pace was slow.

"To tell you the truth, I don't know," the woman said as she went back to braiding the girl's hair.

"Aunt Linda and my mommy went to the . . . ouch!" the girl said, unable to finish telling where her mother had gone. "Grandma, you're pulling my hair too hard."

"Be still and shut your mouth," the woman said, then looked at Tracy. "Why don't you come back tomorrow?"

"Thanks, I will," Tracy said. With slow steps, she walked with Evan to the car.

"You shouldn't walk if you don't have to." Evan opened the door for Tracy.

"You're worse than a little old man. Always worrying."

Evan didn't respond to Tracy's comment. He walked around and got in beside her.

The park was crowded. Rich sounds from the band floated out, filling the air with soulful vibrations. It was impossible to find a parking space, and since he and Tracy didn't have tickets, nor did they know exactly where Linda might be in the park, Evan suggested that they have dinner and wait until morning before calling again.

Tracy noticed that Evan seemed to know his way around the city well enough, especially when he parked and went inside a restaurant advertising home cooking.

A delicious aroma drifted out to them, which smelled like they were inside someone's home, waiting to devour a Sunday dinner. Tracy allowed Evan to help her get seated. She unfolded a blue, floral napkin that matched the tablecloth and took in her surroundings. The room held about twenty tables, all of which were occupied except for a few. The floor was tiled with big blue-and-white squares, and white, ruffled kitchen curtains with tiny blue dots covered the windows.

Tracy was grateful that Evan had come with her now. She was sure that she would've been too exhausted to think about finding food, let alone driving back to Atlanta that night.

She opened her menu and chose the smothered fried chicken and gravy, with white rice and fresh string beans.

"Tracy, I'm starving," Evan announced, ordering fresh green peas, steak smothered in gravy, and smashed potatoes.

Tracy took tiny sips from the ice water the waitress set before them and regarded Evan. As she dwelled on his generosity, she admitted that it was almost impossible to stay angry at him.

"Tracy, I know this might not be the time to discuss this, but I would like to know, why are you holding on to your husband's awards and truck?"

She didn't exactly know how to answer the

question. Nevertheless, she wanted to be honest. At the same time, she didn't know why Evan found it irritating to look at Drake's awards. "Evan, I *am* planning to sell the truck." Tracy said.

"Did you ever think of selling it before now?" Evan asked, forcing her to disclose personal feelings for her deceased husband.

"My intentions were always to sell Drake's truck." She gave Evan her undivided attention. "I guess selling his truck is like losing another part of him."

"Tracy, you can't be in love with a dead man."

"I know, but it was so hard for me." She drank more water, stalling for time, and thinking about how she was going to explain herself to Evan. "Drake was a great part of my life. And what most people don't understand is that, after the funeral and everyone had gone home and gone on with their lives, I didn't stop grieving, just like that." She snapped her fingers.

"There are counseling programs for grief."

"Yes, and I attended a few meetings." She looked at Evan and thought she recognized anguish in his eyes.

"And the certificates?" he continued to question her.

Tracy had almost forgotten about Drake's awards that were hanging on the wall in the study. "Do they bother you?"

"Tracy, you have made me realize that I have feelings for you, that I didn't know I had for anyone." He leaned forward, as if he wanted her to understand his feelings for her. "I already know I love you. But, I can't truly express myself knowing that you don't love me."

"Evan, I *do* love you. But I don't know if we can be friends anymore, not to mention lovers."

"Why?"

"You're involved with a dangerous man on the island who sent you to find me, for a diamond necklace."

"I'm not really involved with him, Tracy. I won't go into it now, but I'll explain it all to you later."

"Are you in trouble with this person?" Tracy asked.

"No, I'm not in trouble. The guy asked me to get the necklace for him, and I told him I would do what I could." He flashed her an unsubdued smile. "When I met you, I was so shocked, I couldn't ask right then. I wanted to get to know you better."

"Who did you expect to find, a wrinkled-up old lady?"

Peals of laughter floated from Evan, turning heads in their direction.

"Baby, to tell you the truth, that was exactly what I expected to find," he said between chuckles.

Tracy waited until the waitress set their food before them, and left the table before she spoke again. "You're as bad as Mrs. Peterson said you were," Tracy announced, knowing now that it really had been Evan who was the mischievous twin.

"Mrs. Peterson." Evan repeated his fourth-grade teacher's name. "She was always checking to see which twin was in her class." He laughed again, lower this time.

"You should've been ashamed of yourself." Tracy smiled at him.

"How the principal knew I was the twin responsible for all the trouble, I'll never know. But when Mrs. Peterson was fed up, she'd send Keith to the office. At least she *thought* it was Keith."

As ridiculous as it was, Tracy laughed. "Why were you in her classroom?" Tracy smiled.

"Girl, my partner was in there."

"It must've been hard, recognizing the differences between you and Keith," Tracy said between small bits of food.

"It was hard to know the difference." Evan grinned. "*You* thought I was Keith."

"I actually thought you were Keith until I checked out your ring finger."

"If I wore a wedding band, you wouldn't know the difference between us."

"I would know."

"How?"

"You talk more than Keith does, and you're not as serious." She giggled. "You also have a tiny mole on the side of your neck."

"You're right. But I'm serious, too."

Tracy smiled at him, and they finished their dinner, pausing occasionally to make small conversation. "You can choose the hotel," Evan said when they finished dinner.

"I don't know Evan, I think we can go home."

"You need to rest."

"Evan, it's not like I broke my leg," Tracy said. One would think she'd just been released from intensive care the way he carried on about her twisted ankle.

"I also think we should share a room, just in case you need my help again tonight."

"Thanks, but I can manage," Tracy said.

"So, now you're afraid to sleep in the same room with me," Evan said as if reading her secret thoughts.

"I didn't say that," Tracy countered.

"You didn't have to say it. I can see it all over your face."

"Evan, think what you want to think," Tracy snapped. He was right. She didn't know if she could sleep in the same room with him without breaking the promises to herself.

"Okay, we'll get one room with double beds. And I'm paying."

"I can pay for myself," Tracy said, not wanting Evan to give her anything.

"*I'm* paying. End of subject." He beckoned for the waitress to bring the bill.

"Why do you have to be in charge of everything?" Tracy argued.

"It's the least I can do, considering it's my fault that we're here."

He has a point, Tracy decided. She wanted to at least pay her half for the hotel room and her food, but without further argument, she went along with Evan's suggestion to pay for her dinner and hotel room. "On second thought, I think I should have my own room," Tracy said, having no desire to take any chances sharing a room with him. After all, once she retrieved the diamond necklace from Linda, and gave it to Evan, their relationship would be over.

"If that's what you want, Tracy," Evan said and got up, walked around to her, and extended his hand in assistance.

Tracy allowed him to help her. It was too bad that their loving relationship hadn't survived. "I need to stop at the store for a few things," Tracy told Evan. She needed a nightgown and bedroom slippers and a small bottle of perfume. She also needed underwear, since she didn't come prepared to spend the night in Augusta.

There was not a gown in the store that Tracy liked. Her intentions were to buy a floor-length gown. The long gowns were sized too big for her. The only ones that fit were the short, baby-doll styles. Reluctantly, Tracy chose a yellow gown and a long yellow housecoat.

The hotel was quiet, cool, and inviting. Tracy sat in one of the round, plush, light-blue chairs while Evan paid for the room. She realized that she was tired. Her ankle twinged lightly with pain, reminding her of the fall. She could have never driven to Augusta and back to Atlanta comfortably without help. The thought crossed her mind as she watched him at the reservation desk, speaking to the clerk.

Evan walked over, and sat in the chair facing her.

"Looks like we'll have to share a room. A double," he announced.

Tracy met Evan's gaze. She had no choice but to share a room with him. She was a determined and strong woman, but she wasn't exactly unaffected by his nearness. The man simply turned her on. But what was she to do, sleep in the car?

"Are you sure that there are no other rooms?" She asked. Evan was not a dishonest person, although he'd sort of forgotten to inform her of important issues.

"You're free to check with the desk clerk," he said.

She noticed him still looking at her, his gaze searching for a reason why she didn't trust that he was being truthful with her.

"All right, I guess we'll have to share a room," Tracy said, maintaining control as the final door to her heart and soul unlocked, promising to release the emotions and compassion she'd stored away. She didn't want to share a room or a bed with Evan. Her reason was simple. She loved him, but after Linda returned the necklace, Tracy wouldn't see Evan again. However, one last night of lovemaking wouldn't be a bad idea.

"We can check out another hotel," Evan offered.

"This hotel is fine," Tracy said. She was too exhausted to travel around, searching for another hotel. She was sure that, with the jazz festival in town, there were no vacancies at any other hotels anyway.

She took one of the pain pills from her purse and swallowed it without water. After a good night's sleep, she was sure that the pain in her ankle would be gone by morning.

Several minutes later, they were in their room. Tracy went over and opened the blinds, unveiling a view of the city. Medium size buildings towered like industrious statues under sapphire lights.

"I'm going to bed," she said, heading to the bathroom to shower and put on the short gown she'd purchased from the store earlier.

"I'll be right back," Evan said.

Tracy was glad that he had left her to her bedtime rituals. She didn't bother to answer or watch as he left her. Never in a million years would she had ever dreamed that she would be attracted to another man besides Drake. Nonetheless, she was aware of her attraction to Evan Maxwell and all of his take-charge control.

His charisma was like gravity, pulling and forcing her against her will to love him. She took a long, hot shower, hoping the hot spray would drench her thoughts and rinse them down the drain, along with the sweet-scented, cherry bath gel.

But her wish was not granted. When she walked out of the bathroom dressed for bed, she noticed that Evan was back. He was lying on the bed face-up, reading the *Augusta Chronicle*. He appeared comfortable, stripped down to his black briefs, exposing strong muscular legs and thighs and his wide, smooth bare chest.

Tracy could've pinched herself for drinking in his gorgeous features. "Where are your clothes?"

she asked, annoyed at herself for allowing Evan's half-naked body to upset her.

"It's too hot to sleep in pajamas." Evan laid the paper on the nightstand, and she noticed that he was smiling.

"And wipe that smile off your face." She heard him chuckle as she turned back the covers and got into her bed.

As soon as she was underneath the covers, Evan sat down at the foot of her bed.

"Tracy, you're a cranky woman tonight. Let me take a look at your ankle," he said, pulling the covers back without her permission. "Does it hurt?" He stroked the area that had been swollen last night.

"It's much better," Tracy said as he massaged her ankle lightly. His touch was soft but powerful as he moved his hand up her leg, stroking her inner thigh. Unable to protest, Tracy relished the caress. His touch rekindled that old, familiar flame.

She gave up on the battle as he covered her lips with a drugging kiss, one that sedated her good sense and ceased all the warning signals— the signals that forewarned her to discontinue with this tryst because it was unrealistic and no good could come from it. She disobeyed the mental counseling and allowed her heart to lead her down a path of passion, edged with scarlet flames that leaped out, striking at will.

While caressing his smooth chest, she kissed him. Evan rose and looked at her, and she knew there would be no turning back. Among the sound of crinkling cellophane and wisps of heady cologne, their worlds collided into the places that only she and Evan knew existed. Like a sizzling torch, she accepted all his glory, and they became one heart, one mind, and one soul.

The next morning, Tracy slipped out of bed while Evan slept. She showered, dressed, and ordered room service, then woke him. "We have to get the necklace from Linda before she goes out again," Tracy said, giving his bare shoulders a light shake.

Evan groaned and rolled over. "I need a few more minutes."

"Then I'll go talk to Linda. You sleep. Okay?"

"Tracy, you are an unmerciful woman," Evan groaned, rolling over and sitting up in bed before he got out and went to take his shower.

Tracy didn't respond to his comment. She went to get their breakfast from the waiter, who was knocking on their door. "Room service!"

Tracy opened the door and let the waiter inside. While he set the food on the dresser, she went to get a tip for him.

"Have a good day," the waiter said, leaving the room.

Tracy heard the water from the shower in the bathroom. She needed to go in and get the perfume she had forgotten to dab on, but she could wait until Evan was finished. She was sure he didn't have the curtains closed, which meant she would have to look at him. Looking at him last night had been the reason for breaking her promise. She had once been able to trust herself and stay in control of a heated situation.

With Evan Maxwell, staying in control was impossible.

Ten minutes later, Evan was out of the bathroom, wearing a towel.

Tracy kept her gaze lowered. "Evan, will you get dressed so we can eat."

He took his pants from the chair where he had left them last night and began to undrape the towel.

"If you don't mind, please go to the bathroom and get dressed," she ordered. They had a diamond necklace to reclaim.

"Tracy, you're a bossy woman, but I love you." Evan said.

Bossy has nothing to do with it, Tracy decided as she waited for the man who set passionate fires inside her.

They finished their breakfast and checked out. Evan was leaving for the island and he was prepared to take the diamond necklace to Frank Johnson. The necklace was the only valuable thing Frank ever owned. His grandmother gave the necklace to him years ago before he'd gone to prison. If Frank had not hid the necklace in the closet in Evan's father's house to keep his uncles from stealing the jewelry, the necklace would never have been sold at the yard sale.

Evan considered that Frank was lucky. Tracy was willing to return the necklace to him. Most people would not have cared, even if they were afraid of what Frank would do to them. Tracy was fair, she could have easily kept the necklace since she paid for the jewelry. If she had paid close attention to the jewelry she could have had the necklace appraised and sold it, and then given the proceeds to the center. Evan mulled over the thought a moment longer. The center seemed to always need money. He decided that Frank was indeed a very lucky man.

Evan parked in front of Linda's sister's house. It appeared that they were still sleeping. The house was quiet, and the children weren't outside. When Tracy smelled bacon frying and coffee brewing, she realized that the family was having breakfast. She knocked on the door.

"Miss Wilson!" Linda was surprised to see her.

"Hi," Tracy said, shifting her weight off her injured ankle.

"How did you hurt yourself?" Linda asked.

"I tripped over a can in the center's parking lot," Tracy replied, not going into details to reveal that Evan had been in the parking lot. She ran thinking he was a thief.

"Did you go the doctor?" Linda asked with concern.

"Yes, and I'll be fine," Tracy assured Linda, trying not to be too anxious about asking for the necklace.

"What brings you to Augusta?" Linda asked.

"I understand that you have a necklace that was in the bag of jewelry I donated to the center," Tracy said. Tracy prayed that Linda had the necklace with her.

"Yes, I do. If I didn't know any better, I'd swear those diamonds were real, Miss Wilson." Linda bragged. "I got so many compliments."

"The necklace is real," Tracy said.

"You're kidding." Linda grinned.

"I'm serious," Tracy said.

"Do I have to give the necklace back?" Linda asked in a pleading voice.

"I'm sorry, Linda, but I need the necklace."

"Miss Wilson, who in the world would put a diamond necklace in a bag of trinkets?"

"Well, Linda, to make a long story short . . ." Tracy said, hobbling over to a nearby chair and sitting down. Her ankle was beginning to throb lightly. "I bought the jewelry from a yard sale while I was on vacation. Later, I learned from my friend that there was a diamond necklace in the bag." Tracy gestured towards Evan who was waiting for her in the car. "The necklace belongs to a man he knows."

"Well—at least I can say I've worn a diamond necklace." Linda smiled.

"Did you bring the necklace with you?" Tracy asked.

"Yes," Linda said. "I'll get it." Linda left Tracy and went inside.

A minute or two later, Linda was back, carrying the open black box displaying a row of sparking diamonds.

"Thank you," Tracy said, relieved that Linda returned the jewelry to her. She braced her hands against the arm of the chair and rose to her feet. The light pain she felt in her ankle before she sat was gone now.

"You're welcome," Linda said.

"Linda, I wish you success with your new job, and don't forget to stop by the center and visit us," Tracy said as she left Linda standing on the porch and went to join Evan, who was waiting for her in the car.

Tracy got in and strapped her seat belt across her. "She didn't want to give it up," she told Evan, handing him the necklace and watching him stick the box in his shirt pocket.

"Thanks, Tracy," Evan said, as they headed back to Atlanta.

Neither one mentioned the previous night's tryst. Tracy was sure that this would be her last time with Evan.

"Tracy, I'll see you when I return from the island," Evan said as he drove toward her house.

"I don't think we should see each other again," Tracy said. She was certain about her feelings for him, but she knew she couldn't continue to date Evan. She still had too many unanswered questions. Their relationship had begun too quickly. The summer wasn't over, and they had already confessed their love for each other. Tracy wanted to make sure she actually loved him, instead of just feeding her starving libido. Then, she was concerned whether or not Evan only wanted to get close to her because of the diamond necklace. After all, their meeting, followed by instant attraction, was all too good to be true.

"No, Tracy, I want us to continue to see each other."

"I think you need to straighten things out on the island first."

"It's not going to be that easy to get rid of me, Tracy."

"Evan, I need time to sort things out for myself," Tracy declared.

"If you need time to get over your husband, I'm not sure I can wait for you to finish grieving."

"There will always be a special place in my heart for Drake." She tried to make him understand.

Evan pulled into her driveway and cut the engine. He turned to her. "I am the only man that's going to have a special place in your heart."

"But Evan—"

"There are no buts, Tracy."

Evan's eyes seemed to brim with an icy chill. She noticed his jaw moving.

"You don't understand."

"I understand that you might be experiencing a little guilt about having feelings for someone other than Drake Wilson."

Tracy's response was to raise her hand to slap Evan.

Evan grabbed her wrist. "You're right, Tracy. You need to get over him."

"I'm trying to move forward, Evan! I don't expect you to wait for me," Tracy said calmly. "In time, I'll be fine." She gathered her purse and the bag she'd put her nightgown in from the backseat. There was nothing more to say to him. She got out and was surprised to see Evan walking a few steps behind her.

"Maybe I'll never understand you, Tracy, but I'll always love you."

Before she could respond, he gathered her in his arms and hugged her tightly.

She nestled against his chest, inhaling his cologne and feeling his strong heartbeat.

He released her, holding her at arm's length. "I'm not rushing you. But, I'm not sharing you with another man, alive *or* dead."

Tracy paid close attention to his serious statement, and she knew that he meant every word. She reached up and kissed his lips lightly. "Good-bye Evan." She stepped out of his embrace, not watching as he walked to his car.

Once inside, she allowed herself to cry. This time her tears were not for Drake. Because of Drake, she had lost Evan.

Tracy knew she had to make serious changes. Because of her grip on the past, she had lost Evan. And she couldn't blame him. If he had a deceased wife and had held on to her personal possessions, she would be upset, too. At that moment, she realized that she had made a big mistake. She'd let Evan go. Now, it was too late for them.

Sixteen

Blue ocean waves rolled to shore on the sandy white beach, while motors from speed boats blustered, intermingling with the echos of sea gulls fishing for a noonday treat. Evan walked out of his ocean condo to the harbor, and unanchored his boat. This would be his final visit to Frank Johnson. The man would soon be out of his life forever. Evan was thankful that Tracy had been lucky enough to retrieve the necklace. With a little more time, Linda might have realized that the diamond necklace actually had genuine gems. Evan didn't want to speculate about what might have happened if the woman became aware of the small fortune she was holding.

As he sped across the water to Frank's house, his mind turned to Tracy. It was better that they had broken off their relationship. He didn't know how much more he could stand. He was so jealous of her late husband that he barely knew what to do. He had hated Drake Wilson the night he went into her study and saw the awards on the wall. Even in death, the man monopolized Tracy's heart. Evan wasn't a man to give up easily. But he also knew when to throw in his cards, and he wasn't playing the game anymore.

Evan pushed these thoughts to the back of his mind. Just thinking that he'd competed with a dead man and lost was making him angry.

He had kept himself busy when he returned to the island. Before he left Atlanta, he and Keith stopped by their mother's house, and she would not let them leave until they promised to check into the letter she'd received from their father's lawyer. Evan had taken the letter, and Keith agreed to return with him to the St. Hope Isle. They both were sure that their father hadn't made a mistake. Baily Maxwell had been a thorough man in all his undertakings. Evan was absolutely positive that their father had left the woman they thought he had married something of value. But according to the letter, everything went to their mother. Still, none of it made sense.

Evan pressed the gas pedal, moving the speed boat faster across the water. Houses hiding between tall palms soon came into view. Women stood on shore under flaxen-and-maroon tents, braiding and slipping colorful beads onto tourists' hair.

Evan slowed the boat as he headed toward the tiny community where Frank lived. He noticed a skinny teenage boy running toward him. Evan knew the boy wanted to anchor his boat—for a small fee. He got out and allowed the boy to take care of the vessel, even though he knew he would only be spending a few minutes with Frank.

"He's not home." A woman walked over to Evan and stood at the edge of Frank's yard.

"Do you know when he'll be back?" Evan asked, annoyed that he had wasted his time bringing the diamond necklace to Frank, especially since Frank had been adamant about him returning the piece of jewelry. Evan knew he should've called Frank before he drove over to his house. He returned to the boat, took some paper from the pad in the boat's compartment, and wrote Frank a message: CALL ME WHEN YOU GET HOME. I HAVE A PACKAGE FOR YOU.

As soon as Evan returned to his apartment, he and Keith went to Baily's lawyer's office to make sure no mistakes had been made in the will.

It didn't take long to sort out the confusion. Their father had left his business and holdings to their mother, with the distinct warning that if she remarried, she would then turn the business over to their sons. Evan and Keith also learned that their father had never married the woman their mother referred to as the "siren woman." However, he did leave the other woman a sizable amount of money, stating that since she'd nursed him through his illness, it was fair to see that she was financially secure. However, he felt safe leaving his holdings to Mavis, who was a businesswoman.

Evan smiled to himself when he thought that maybe their father had still loved their mother. It seemed obvious to Evan since his father had given their mother the private club after they were separated. It wasn't as if she needed the club. She owned a successful dress factory.

When the company where she started out as a seamstress—and was finally promoted to supervisor, then to manager—was going out of business, their mother borrowed money from their father and bought the factory. She paid their father back every cent of the money, as promised.

Thinking about his parents' relationship brought memories of Tracy to his mind. He wanted to hold her, talk to her, and love her. But he couldn't. Tracy was not interested in loving him.

For the better part of the day, Evan worked. When he took a break, he reached for his phone and automatically dialed Tracy's number at work. She answered, and he hung up. Their relationship was over; they had both agreed.

Regardless of the mutual agreement, he still loved her. He needed time to forget.

Seventeen

Tracy and Regina returned from their land-sale seminar sooner than expected. She had kept quiet about her break up with Evan. It was bad enough that when she thought about Evan, she wanted to fly to the island to be with him. Then there was Keith, who was Evan's mirror image. Tracy avoided any contact with him unless it was an emergency.

Tracy went to her office. While she checked her listing appointments for the rest of the week, Regina's phone rang. After the second ring, Tracy answered the call.

"Hi, Tracy. Is Regina around?" Grant's voice reached out to her.

"No, she's not in the office at the moment, but she'll be in soon," Tracy said to him, wondering if he knew she and Evan had broken up.

"Will you tell her to call me?"

"Yes, I will," Tracy agreed, immediately reaching for a pen to write a message to leave on Regina's desk, in case she forgot to tell her that Grant called.

Tracy took the message and hung up the

phone, forbidding herself to think. If she did, she would think about Evan.

As she went back to work, Keith knocked on the office door and walked in before she could invite him.

"How are you?" Keith asked with concern.

"I'm fine," Tracy said, glancing at him briefly. Her instincts warned her not to look at the exact image of her ex-lover.

Keith's lips edged into a smile. "I understand that things are going well at the center."

"Yes," Tracy replied, keeping her answers short.

"It was very generous of Evan to donate the computers."

"Yes, it was," Tracy answered. "We are very thankful."

"Have you talked to him lately?"

"No, I haven't."

Keith's smile developed into a full-blown grin. He reached into his suit pocket and took out an envelope. "Maybe this will help the program." He walked over to her and dropped the envelope on Tracy's desk.

"Thanks, Keith, I'll give it to Janet," Tracy said, wondering why Keith hadn't mailed the check to the Women in Need of Help office.

"You're welcome," Keith said and walked out of her office.

Tracy brushed the concerns regarding Keith's action out of her mind. She had work to do. But Keith's interest in her and Evan bothered her, and memories of Evan tugged at her mind.

Tracy closed the folder and pushed away from

her desk. If she wanted Evan, she had to make him aware of her feelings. It wasn't that she was still in love with Drake. She simply cherished the memories they once shared.

Tracy dialed Evan's office on St. Hope Isle, knowing that her actions were braver than she felt. But she had to speak to him, if for no other reason than to let him know that she cared.

His secretary answered on the first ring, telling her that Evan was not in the office but she would have him call her.

Tracy graciously thanked the secretary and resumed her work, putting the thought of Evan out of her mind. Before she even realized it, it was almost five o'clock. She left the office with plans to stop by the center to give Keith's donation to Janet. She also wanted to know how the masquerade party arrangements were proceeding, which was planned for that Saturday night. Tracy decided to save herself the trouble of getting stuck in traffic and called Janet once she arrived home. She would drop Keith's donation check off the following day.

She called Janet, learning that everything was set for the party, including the food that Hannah had agreed to donate.

Still holding the receiver, Tracy dialed Evan's home number on the island. She was certain that he wasn't home yet, but she was also aware that he listened to his messages.

"Hello?" A woman's voice answered Evan's phone.

"I would like to speak to Evan," Tracy said,

wondering if she had the right number. According to Evan, he was single and free . . . or had he found another lover as quickly as he'd found her?

"Why do you want to speak to Evan?" the woman asked.

Tracy felt her blood heating, as if hot stones lay heavy in her chest.

"Will you give him a message?"

"And what would that be?"

"Just tell him to call Tracy."

"Sure, as soon as we return from dinner."

Tracy eased the phone down onto the receiver. She should have known better than to call him.

But she had, and now she knew Evan was serious when they had their last argument. She quickly dismissed Evan Maxwell, and busied herself making labels for her moving boxes.

Life was too precious to pine over a man who didn't have the decency to let the love affair cool off before he dated again. Salty tears stung her eyes. Evan Maxwell was an unscrupulous man, to say the least.

On Saturday afternoon, Shun removed the last gold-framed award from the study's wall and handed it to Tracy, who carefully wrapped it. For the last time, she said good-bye to Drake. A tear spilled and slid down her cheek.

"Tracy, is everything okay?" Shun asked.

"It's hard to say good-bye, Shun."

"I can imagine it is. Drake was a good guy."

"Yes, he was." Tracy lay the award in the box with the others. Drake had been honest and forthright. He wasn't a saint, but at least he never played with her emotions. If he made her a promise, he tried to keep it. And if he couldn't keep his promises, he had a straightforward explanation. That's why she had loved him, and for that reason, there would always be a special place in her heart for him, whether Evan liked it or not.

"You know what I don't understand, Tracy?"

"What don't you understand, Shun?"

"How can you be in love with Evan and still love Drake."

Tracy started not to respond to Shun's immature evaluation. "I never told you that I was in love with Evan."

"You don't have to tell me." Shun dropped down on the sofa. "Actions speak louder than words."

Tracy was aware of her feelings for Evan and knew she was too old for infatuations. Shun was right. She loved Evan, but now it was too late.

"Shun, Evan and I aren't even seeing each other anymore." She spoke quickly.

"Too bad Mom and Dad didn't get a chance to meet him," Shun replied.

Tracy glanced at him. She was glad she hadn't introduced Evan to Hannah and Jordan. She wanted to make sure of the relationship before she introduced him to any other family members. It was coincidence that Shun had met him.

"Anyway, Shun, if you're going to the masquerade party, you better get home and get dressed."

After Shun left, Tracy went upstairs to get ready for the party and wrangle with the tears that threatened to spill. Her first tears had been for Drake, and now they were for Evan. She had lost the two men she loved.

Tracy lay across her bed and cried. She would gain the strength to move on. She promised herself that she would remember not to move too swiftly concerning the affairs of the heart. She allowed Evan to engulf her spirit, and even Shun knew she loved him—and she did, no matter how she denied her emotions. It was true. Just like Drake, Evan was gone—only Evan was alive and sharing what they'd had with another woman. She could almost taste the green jealousy rising from the pit of her stomach.

The phone rang. Tracy rose and answered it. When she heard Evan's voice, she slowly lowered the receiver back onto the cradle. She couldn't think of anything to say to him, and even if she could, she didn't want him to hear the tears in her voice.

She got up and braided her hair into several medium-sized braids and went to take a long, hot bath. As she soaked in aromatic bubbles, she discarded each thought relating to her and Evan that tipped across her mind. She finished her bath and rinsed herself off with cool water, allowing the braids to dampen. Tracy dried off, slipped into her thick, white, terry housecoat and took her hair dryer from the closet. She sat until her braids were dry.

Tracy took a dress from the closet and examined it for what seemed like the third or fourth time that week. It had a low back that stopped at her waist—perfect for the warm weather, not to mention sexy. She put the dress on and slipped into a pair of black high heels. Tracy sat at her vanity and unwound the braids, satisfied with her long, wavy tresses. She arranged the spiral strands with her fingers, misting her hair with holding spray and adding a small amount of oil sheen. The waves hung loosely over her bare back. Tracy clipped on a pair of clustered diamond earrings that Hannah had given to her for her last birthday. She dabbed on her favorite perfume, and headed out to her car.

At Hannah's, white linen cloths covered round tables accented with gold centerpieces. Palm trees and tropical plants adorned the corners. The stage had been decorated for Janet and the other speakers. It appeared that the party company went all out with gold, black, and white balloons.

Tracy took her place at the door, greeting guests.

"Girlfriend, we have to talk later tonight." Regina came in and stood beside Tracy. Her red, ruffled dress made her look as if she'd just stepped out the eighteenth century. Regina held up a black lace fan and began fanning herself as if imaginary heat overwhelmed her.

"Regina, who are you suppose to be with that wig piled up on your head?"

"I don't know," Regina said with a Southern drawl. "But I do know one thing. I'm crazy about Mr. Grant."

"So, where is he?" Tracy wanted know. She knew that if Grant had received an invitation to the party, Evan might attend as well. Tracy remembered that Janet had mentioned she was inviting the people who had made donations.

"He's outside talking to Evan and Keith."

"Oh."

"Is that all you have to say?"

Tracy was glad to see another couple enter the room. "Hello," she spoke to them, admiring their Cinderella and prince costumes, instead of responding to Regina's question.

"Are you volunteering your services tonight?" Tracy asked Regina, who was acting as if she never had a boyfriend before.

"I'm donating my time to Grant tonight . . . sorry." She wheeled around and moved to the door, hooking her arm in Grant's as he, Evan, and Keith walked inside.

Tracy nodded at Keith who was dressed as Dracula; his wife was a beautiful maiden.

"The outfit is perfect," Tracy said and laughed.

"Are you trying to tell me something?" Keith grinned.

"Go figure it out," Tracy smiled, trying to ignore Evan's presence as he eased up beside her.

It was almost impossible, especially when she noticed that he was only wearing a black jacket, pants, and a gold chain. To top that off, Evan wore a black patch over his eye.

"Can you get someone to cover for you?" Evan asked her in a low voice while she smiled and greeted the guests.

"No," she said, still smiling.

"Tracy, baby." Barry walked in dressed in a black tux, wearing a top hat, and carrying a cane.

"Barry, you look absolutely wonderful." Tracy admired his costume.

"Don't forget our date." Barry leaned over and kissed Tracy's cheek.

"I need to talk to you." Evan whispered.

"Hi." Tracy spoke to a couple that entered, ignoring Evan's whisper. She didn't know what Evan wanted to talk to her about. He had his diamond necklace. Maybe he wanted to tell her about the woman that was now living with him. She felt a jealous rage rise inside her, and she wanted Evan to go away. "We don't have anything to talk about."

She noticed Evan pushing his hands down in his trouser pockets, moving closer to her. He smelled good. Fresh, clean soap, mingled with his cologne, was enough to disarm her anger. His closeness and masculine aroma almost drove her to stop greeting the guests and find out what important message he had for her.

"We're talking tonight, whether you want to or not," Evan warned her, and walked into the dining room.

Tracy didn't challenge him. She continued to greet people as they entered the room, giving them their seating passes before they were shown to their tables.

"I'll take over." Betty said from behind her.

"Ooh, I love the dress." Tracy admired the tight, black dress with a thick, ruffled split up the side that exposed Betty's shapely legs.

"Thank you, darling. You're looking cute yourself." Betty nudged Tracy so she would move away from the stand.

Tracy hurried through the dining room to find Janet. When she didn't see her, Tracy went to the office. Janet was there, speaking to Hannah. She wore a long, white, dress with ruffled sleeves and a Brussel back. The gathered lace material covering her hip made Janet appeared as if she'd stepped off a stagecoach.

"What is this?" Tracy tugged at the ruffles around Janet's hips.

"I couldn't resist renting it." Janet laughed.

Tracy turned to Hannah. She wore a black, flared, short-sleeve dress, black heels and a pair of diamond earrings. "Hi," Tracy spoke. "I think we should get started."

"I think so, too," Hannah agreed with Tracy.

Dinner was soon served. The chef had prepared prime rib with all the trimmings. Tracy decided that she would sit with Hannah, Jordan, and Barry.

She had scarcely joined them when she felt a strong pair of hands on her waist, turning her around. "Let's go to the office." Evan's eyes seemed to darken.

Jordan, Barry, and Hannah rose from their seats as Tracy spoke. "Everyone, this Evan Maxwell. He's responsible for the center receiving the computers. He's also a friend," she added, not wanting her family to think that she and Evan were on the verge of a fight.

Evan extended his hand to Jordan and then to Hannah. "It's good to meet you."

"Yes." Hannah smiled, and Jordan nodded his approval.

"And this is Barry," Tracy said, noticing that Evan had ignored him.

"We met at the door," Evan said to her. He put his hand on her waist. "Please excuse us. Tracy and I have business to attend too."

To prevent a scene, Tracy led Evan to Hannah and Jordan's office.

"What do you want?" Tracy asked once they were alone.

"You couldn't wait before you got yourself a new boyfriend?"

"*I* couldn't wait?" Tracy shot back at him. "Barry is a good friend, and I know you're not upset with me because you think I have a lover, Evan," Tracy said.

"I don't want another man slobbering on my woman," Evan said.

"*Your* woman. Now, would that be me, or the little Jezebel in St. Hope Isle answering your home phone?"

She watched the expression change on his face. "What?"

"Forget it, Evan." Tracy was moving back to the door when his grasp stopped her.

Tracy backed away from him and rested her hips on the edge of the desk, fighting to forget the memories of his touch, his kiss, and the haunting memories of his lovemaking. She finally looked at him. "First, you had a problem with me holding a special place in my heart for Drake. However, that didn't stop you from living with another woman."

"Tracy what're talking about?"

"I believed you when you told me you were single." She lifted her gaze to watch his expression.

"There's no one in my life."

She heard his protest, but she continued to lash out at him. "Evan, in my opinion, living together is like being married." She swallowed her salty tears. "You just don't have a marriage license."

Evan grabbed her shoulders, pushing her further against the desk. "Tracy, that's not true."

Tracy placed her hands on his chest and pushed against him, freeing herself. She could feel her tears rising again as she responded with tart defiance. But then she composed herself, not wanting him to see her pain.

"I don't play games, Tracy, and I live alone." Evan protested quietly.

"Sure you do, Evan, when you're living in an Atlanta hotel."

"Listen to me, Tracy." He reached out and folded his arms around her.

Tracy held up her hands. "Get off me." He released her, and she almost ran from the office, leaving him inside. She held on to the door knob, slowly pulling the door behind her to keep from slamming it. From the small crack, she heard him curse.

Evan sank down in Hannah's chair, resting his head against the soft, black leather back, and stared at the ceiling. He was surprised that Tracy had even called him. He and Grant had been too busy. So busy that he had asked his secretary to send one of the clerks over to his place and unlock his apartment door for the new cleaning woman. Because the regular cleaning lady was unable to work that particular day, the woman replacing her didn't have a key. He also instructed his secretary to have the clerk return when the maid finished her work. The clerk was to give the woman the check and lock his apartment.

Evan touched his mustache, rubbing his finger over the edge of his lip. The clerk? Evan wondered. She had to be the one who answered his phone. The cleaning woman was older. He felt his blood race, remembering how the young girl had called one of his male employee's home and conveniently lied to his wife. The poor man was upset because his wife threw him out the house. Evan remembered speaking to him regarding his poor work performance, and he learned that the clerk was at the root of the problem.

If I find out that she was the person who answered my telephone, she better start looking for another job, because I'm firing her. With that thought in mind, Evan got up and went out to join the festivities.

He only heard half of what Janet and the others were saying while making their speeches. The prime rib tasted like wood as far as he was concerned. Although he was sure the food was delicious, he had lost his appetite. For the entire evening, he watched Tracy enjoy herself talking to Barry, who didn't seem to miss an opportunity to give her all of his attention. It had been a long time since Evan experienced misery in its rawest form.

As the evening drew to an end, couples were having the last dance. Evan wouldn't let himself leave without holding Tracy and inviting her to the island to spend a weekend. He had to show her that he was single and free—and most of all that he loved her.

Evan walked over to the table where Tracy was engaged in a conversation with Barry and the others. He took her hand, and without asking, drew her up in his arms and led her out on the floor. He could tell from her quiet reaction that she wasn't pleased, but he wasn't concerned. He drew her to him and held her tight. She felt good against him as he placed his lips close to her ear.

"I want you to come to the island and visit with me next weekend." When she didn't answer him, he wasn't exactly satisfied, but she had to understand that he wasn't giving up.

When the music stopped, Evan walked with her back to her table and left the party. He had a problem to solve back home and he meant to do it as soon as possible. In the meantime, he hoped this would give Tracy time to decide if she would accept his invitation. If she refused, he wouldn't like her decision, but he'd have to live with it.

Eighteen

"Tracy, what's going on with you and Evan?" Regina asked.

Tracy didn't look up from the contract she'd filled out earlier that morning. She didn't answer Regina's question or attempt to discuss her and Evan's problem.

"Tracy?"

"Regina, I don't want to discuss Evan." She did want to acccpt his invitation to visit him on the island. Tracy also wanted to believe him when he told her he didn't have a lover. But she was ambivalent. If she visited Evan, she would be admitting that she was interested in a long-distance relationship. If she chose not to accept his invitation, she would miss the opportunity to relax and enjoy herself. She placed the client's contract inside the folder and deposited her uncertainties in the back recesses of her mind.

"But Tracy, can't you and Evan work out your problem?" Regina probed. "I was looking forward to spending the weekend on the island with Grant, you, and Evan."

"Regina, I never told you that Evan and I had a problem."

"Tracy, it's clear for anyone to see. You were angry with him the night of the party."

"It's none of your business, but Evan and I aren't seeing each other anymore."

Regina got up and walked to the door. "It's up to you if you want to stay in Atlanta and feel sorry for yourself. But I'm going to St. Hope Isle."

"You should go and enjoy yourself. After all, you and Grant are lovers."

"Evan can't be that bad, Tracy," Regina shot back.

"Regina, shut up. You don't know what you're talking about."

"Oh, yeah?" Regina snapped. "You're too stubborn to admit that you're in love with the man."

"I never said I didn't love him," Tracy said. "You don't know what happened."

"Then tell me because I'd like to know."

"No," Tracy said, snatching another folder from the tray.

"Well, keep your business to yourself then."

Tracy considered Regina's argument, then turned her attention back to her work.

"Ladies, ladies!" Barry walked in the office, smiling at Tracy and Regina. "I assume you lovely creatures are having a cat fight." Barry looked distinguished as ever, dressed in an expensive suit.

"Shut up Barry," Tracy and Regina said in unison.

Barry laughed and held up his hands in mock defense. "Tracy, I stopped by for two reasons."

"And they are?"

"I would like to take you to lunch, and I would like to show one of your listings."

"Yes, you can show my listing and sell it." She pushed away from her desk and stood. "And no, I can't have lunch with you."

"Okay. I'll go get the keys from the secretary."

"Sure, Barry," Tracy said. "Let me give you the check for my condo." She took out her checkbook and wrote a check for him.

"Thanks, Tracy, I'll get this to the broker, and we should close within two weeks."

"You're buying a condo?" Regina inquired.

"Yes, I am."

"Tracy, why didn't you tell me?"

"Because I didn't think you needed to know," Tracy remarked. She was more upset with herself about the predicament she'd gotten herself into with Evan than she was with Regina for wanting to know every detail concerning her personal life.

"Tracy, when you find your good sense, we'll talk." Regina walked out and closed the door with a quick snap.

Tracy covered her face with her hands. *Lord, please don't let me lose my mind,* she thought. Regina was more like a sister than a best friend. At least once every six months, they got into a verbal fight. It didn't matter what the argument was about. But it usually concerned a choice one of them had made. In this case, Tracy had chosen not to see Evan anymore, and Regina was upset. However, her reaction toward Regina wasn't good. She had to make it up to her.

The next day, Tracy had still not decided whether or not she would accept Evan's invitation. Nevertheless, the more she thought about the beautiful island and its white, sandy beaches—and the boutiques and shopping—the more difficult it became to ignore Evan's invitation. She knew that if she continued to think about the beautiful island, she would eventually talk herself into going. She was still hesitant. She had loved and trusted Evan, only to learn that he was involved in a serious relationship on the island. *Or is he?* Tracy mused. The confusion trapped her. Had she been so starved for affection that she accepted the first man that came along?

She had been careful for a long time. She wasn't exactly waiting for the right man to sweep her off her feet. However, Evan did just that. She couldn't forget the obsession that Evan released in her. He slipped into her life like a whirlwind, spinning and weaving his way into her world. As a result, her emotions were tangled, and she didn't doubt it would take a very long time to untangle the web.

That evening, when Tracy checked her calendar, she saw there weren't any pressing appointments for the day. She needed to talk to someone, but she wasn't talking to Regina. Usually Hannah had the right advice although Tracy didn't always take her sister's recommendation.

Today, she first needed to know how Hannah would handle this situation.

Ten minutes later, Tracy rang Hannah's doorbell. While she waited patiently for her sister to open the door, she took in the peaceful atmosphere surrounding Hannah and Jordan's home: the begonias with dark green leaves and white blooms sitting on rich green grass; a bluebird, perching atop a small pine at the corner of Hannah's lawn, fluttering its wings and preparing to take flight. Tracy marveled at the peace, wishing that one day her life would be as wholesome and happy as Hannah's.

"Come in, Tracy." Hannah said.

The house was cooler than outside but held the same serenity Tracy had experienced before she entered.

"Let me get us a glass of tea," Hannah offered as Tracy followed her to the kitchen.

Tracy sat at the round table and toyed with a leaf on the flower centerpiece. Ice clattered as Hannah filled a glass.

"All right, what did he do to get you this upset?" Hannah set the iced tea on the table and sat across from Tracy.

"Did I say he . . . Hannah?"

"Tracy, the way the two of you were carrying on the night of the party, it goes without saying that something is wrong." No matter how calm Tracy appeared, she could never fool Hannah.

Tracy took a tiny sip of the dark tea Hannah set in front of her. She didn't realize that she and Evan had been so obvious, not even after Regina had mentioned their behavior. "Evan wants me to spend the weekend with him on the island." Tracy knew that she didn't need Hannah's permission, but after she explained the situation, she wondered what Hannah would do if she were confronted with a similar decision. "I don't know what to do."

Hannah raised an eyebrow at her and remained silent for a short while before she spoke. "Why aren't you shopping and packing and confirming your flight reservation?"

"I don't think Evan is serious about us."

"Why do you think he's not serious?"

Tracy explained how another woman had answered Evan's phone.

"Tracy, remember when I thought Jordan was having an affair? I was fit to be tied. And you gave me very good advice. At least you made me think, and you were right."

"But this is different."

"How?" Hannah asked her. "Except for the fact that you aren't married to him, there's no difference."

Tracy was quiet as she considered her sister's observation. She still wasn't certain if she should accept Evan's invitation. "I'll think about it," she finally said, finishing her tea.

Their conversation turned in a more casual direction. Hannah told Tracy that Jordan was taking her to Jamaica after she completed her college courses at the end of the summer. Since Jordan had learned to dance, they planned to party until dawn.

Tracy laughed, thinking how Jordan's dance lessons almost had him in divorce court.

"I'm selling my house," Tracy said then, telling Hannah about her reasons to sell.

"I'm glad, Tracy," Hannah said. "Sometimes I worry about you living alone in that big house."

"I found this wonderful condo, and I should be moving in soon."

"Good. Shun told me that you were selling the truck, too."

"I need to move on," Tracy said. If Evan was never in her life again, she still couldn't stay stuck in the past.

"Change takes time, and you can't rush it." Hannah smiled. "You're ready to go forward."

Tracy nodded in agreement. As usual, Hannah was right. "Hannah, I'll see you later this week."

"I want you to call me from St. Hope Isle, let me know that you arrived safely."

"If I decide to accept Evan's invitation, I'll give you a call."

Nineteen

Evan stood in the center of his office, gazing out at the ocean through the open blinds and trying to decide if he should take his secretary's advice and not fire the clerk. He wanted to fire the young woman right away. He continued to stare out his office window, as if the view held some mysterious answer to his decision.

Waves rippled lightly against the wind, and boats that resembled tiny toys sped across the water. Even with the window closed, he could hear a fishing barge honking as it pulled into a distant port.

Evan moved closer to the window and allowed his mind to wander, digesting the last time he tried to convince Tracy of his innocence. She seemed adamant about her decision. He hoped that she would change her mind and spend the weekend with him.

He rubbed his hand over his face and went to his secretary's office. "I want you in my office when I talk to the clerk," he said. He'd learned from the maid that the clerk had answered Tracy's call.

"We'll be right in," the secretary said.

Evan went back to his office, leaving the door open while he waited. He began to consider the secretary's plea. If he fired the clerk, she wouldn't be able to help her mother, her younger sister, and her brother. According to the secretary, the clerk needed the job.

"We're here for the meeting," the secretary said as she and the clerk entered Evan's office.

"I'm sorry, I didn't mean to say those things to the woman that called you," the clerk started before Evan could address the subject. He imagined that the secretary had clued her in on what the meeting was about.

"How do you think I should solve this problem?" Evan asked, noticing the clerk's guilty conscience. He didn't want to waste much time on her, since he had decided not to dismiss her.

The nineteen-year-old clerk was barely out of high school and should have been attending college, instead of playing telephone games.

"I don't know, but I don't want to be fired. I'm sorry," she cried.

Evan turned to his secretary. "When do the next professional image and human-relation classes begin?"

"The first class begins tomorrow night. I'll check and see if it is full," the secretary offered.

"Sign her up."

"But I can't. I've made plans for this week after work," the young lady explained, sounding close to tears.

"You have a choice," Evan said, "You can take the classes, or I can fire you."

"I'll take the classes," the clerk said, not looking at Evan or the secretary.

"Good choice," Evan said.

The women left his office, and Evan attempted to get back to work and not call Tracy. He wanted her to come to him because *she* wanted him, not because she felt obligated to do him a favor.

All day, Evan worked hard. It was his way of keeping his mind free from thinking about Tracy. However, it only worked half the time. Otherwise, his mind wandered to her, and he found himself wanting to call her. But calling Tracy might only make matters worse. She was stubborn, outspoken, confident, and angry at him.

When Evan couldn't stand another minute, he picked up the receiver and held it, almost breaking his promise, before forcing himself to set it back on the cradle and going back to his work. Then the phone rang. Evan pushed the speaker button and answered the call. "Maxwell, how can I help you."

"I'm back," An English voice said, loud and clear.

"Who is this?" Evan asked.

"Evan, it's Wanda."

Evan recognized his ex-girlfriend's voice. "Yeah?"

"I'm sorry to say it, but I made a mistake."

"What mistake did you make, Wanda?"

"I made a mistake about us," she said.

Evan looked at the telephone. "Wanda, things between us are good the way they are."

"You don't want to see me."

"Right."

"But Evan, I just needed time to think."

Evan didn't say anything. He stared at the receiver. He hadn't thought about Wanda since she said that she was in love with a man in England. "I have to go." Evan paused with his finger over the speaker button.

"Evan . . ."

He pushed the button, shutting her out. Tracy Wilson was the only woman that mattered to him.

Late that afternoon, when Grant told him that he was going to the airport to pick up Regina, Evan knew that Tracy wouldn't be coming along.

"We'll see you later, right?" Grant asked Evan.

"No, I think I'll stay in tonight," Evan replied. He didn't envy Grant's happiness. He was sorry that he'd ruined his relationship with Tracy. He wanted her to forget her deceased husband, but he detested feeling like he was competing with him for her love. He was so jealous of Drake Wilson. Except for that, it was as if his involvement with her was doomed from the very beginning.

He had been surprised when he met her, and she had dazzled him from the very beginning with her good looks and intelligence. From that moment on, his promise to Frank seemed to evaporate into thin air. He was in love.

At the end of the day, Evan went home. He didn't bother to turn on the lights, eat, or change into a comfortable pair of shorts as he usually did when he arrived home from work.

He lay on the sofa, freeing his mind of all thoughts. There was nothing to think about now but work, and he *didn't* want to think about work.

He got up and pulled off his shirt, and threw it on a nearby chair. Then he laid down and stretched out again. His eyes felt tired. He got up again, this time taking some eyedrops from the cabinet in the bathroom and squeezing a few drops into his eyes. Then, he put on the black patch and resumed his position on the sofa. Finally, he dozed but was soon abruptly drawn out of a fitful sleep, thinking he'd heard the doorbell. When he didn't hear the bell again, he assumed that he was dreaming and closed his eyes. The bell rang again, and this time he knew it was not his imagination. It was probably Frank coming for the necklace. If it was Wanda, she wasn't getting in.

Evan got up slowly and moved at a snail's pace to open the door. He didn't even bother to look through the tiny round peephole. He opened the door.

"Tracy." He couldn't believe she was standing before him. She looked beautiful, dressed in black, wide-leg linen pants and a black halter top with bare-backed shoes. He pulled her inside, wrapping her in his arms, and kissed her. When she returned his kiss, he knew that they were meant to be together.

Frank Johnson returned from the legitimate job he'd been hired to do, which was working on a fishing barge. He'd been gone for a while and doubted that Evan had returned from the States with the diamond necklace. He decided that he would stick to his original plan and fly to Atlanta. If he wanted the necklace, he'd have to get it himself.

Twenty

There was no need for greetings or words. The sensations racing between Evan and Tracy spoke volumes. Tracy savored Evan's lingering kiss and their mutual passion. She was no longer angry at him but completely satisfied that she'd made the right choice to spend her weekend with him.

Tracy pulled away and out of another one of Evan's sedating kisses, which seemed to calm every fiber in her heart, but at the same time unleashed a zealous thirst.

"Perhaps we should save all of this until after dinner," Tracy suggested. "I'm starving."

Evan gave her one last hug before releasing her entirely. "I'll be back shortly," he said.

She watched him trot out of the room and vanish through the entrance that led to the hallway. She assumed that he was going to shower, dress, and then take her to dinner. She looked around the living room, absorbing her surroundings. The room was much like Evan's personality. It was light and airy, with wide windows. A black statue added a hint of mysterious danger to the decor. The sofa and chair were overstuffed, light-gray leather. A gigantic spider plant, draped in a red clay pot, hung from a silver bookshelf.

She walked over to the shelf and studied the rows of books. Near the end of the shelf, she found and stroked a white-and-blue model speed boat. Tracy speculated that Evan's passion must have been for boats because a picture of the same boat hung on the wall. As she studied the room, she saw no signs that a woman also shared the space.

More than ten minutes later, Evan joined her. The fresh scent of soap and his cologne made her heart tingle. He wore dark-blue slacks and a thin beige shirt, which made him more attractive than ever. Tracy noticed that he was once again wearing the black eye patch over his eye. She had thought that when he attended the masquerade party the black eye patch was part of his costume. "Evan, do you have problems with your eye?" she asked.

"I have a slight problem," he said, slipping his arm around her waist and walking with her to the door.

Tracy stopped walking. "When did it happen?"

"Tracy, I'll tell you about it soon," he promised as they left his apartment.

Tracy was still curious as she waited for him to lock the door, but she decided not to press him for information. She wanted to enjoy herself—and him—tonight and the entire weekend.

They walked down the pier to Evan's boat. Tracy got in beside him, and they rode further down the ocean to a part of the island that Tracy had not visited during her first excursion to the island.

Lights glittered against the water like chipped rainbow pieces. Tall buildings rose above a smooth concert sidewalk. Further down, people dined at an outside restaurant. Tracy took in the sights as she and Evan left his boat to be docked.

Evan covered her hand with his as they sauntered across the pier and seated themselves at a table overlooking the ocean.

Tracy was enjoying herself. The winds lifted her hair, and the scent of delicious food and the sound of music wafted through the fresh air. "This is pure heaven," Tracy said, more to herself than to Evan.

"Tracy, I tried to return the necklace to Frank, but he wasn't home," Evan told her once they had settled down and ordered their dinner and wine.

"I hope you have it stored in a safe place, because I don't want that man stalking me."

"The necklace is in my safe," Evan assured her.

"Whew!" Tracy brushed her forehead as if she were wiping away beads of perspiration. "You know, Evan, he is a crazy man. The day I bought that bag of jewelry from the woman, I think he followed me."

"He could've followed you. It sounds like a trick he would pull."

"I'm not sure," Tracy added. "He was tall,

with very light skin, and his teeth were really big."

"That was Frank," Evan confirmed.

"He attended the hotel party." Tracy began to tell Evan the details of the evening she'd attended the hotel party.

"Did you speak to him?"

Tracy shrugged. "Yes. I told him I thought he had followed me earlier, and he said no."

"Tracy, when you're in a strange place, you have to be careful," Evan warned her.

"I *was* careful." Tracy said, remembering how she'd excused herself and went to her room. "All he had to do was ask for the necklace, and I would have given it to him."

"I don't want anything to happen to you," Evan said, with a far-away look in his eyes.

"I have to take care of a few things tomorrow. You can use the boat if you want to."

"Thank you." Tracy smiled. She hadn't driven a boat in years. Drake had encouraged her to get a license. She had enjoyed riding along the Savannah coast with Drake, Hannah, and Jordan.

"But, you must be careful," Evan warned her again.

"I promise." Tracy laughed, holding up one hand.

"There are pirates on the ocean, Tracy, and I don't want you to be harmed."

"Okay, I'll stay close to the beach." Tracy detected concern in Evan's voice.

Evan frowned. "And stay away from those houses farther down the beach."

"But Evan, those homes are nice."

"Tracy."

"Okay. I'll go shopping, and I won't stop to sightsee."

A waiter dressed in black set their seafood on the table, along with a carafe of wine.

Tracy tasted her shrimp, which was seasoned with a spicy butter sauce, before she added yellow rice to the tender meat.

"Enjoy your dinner," the waiter said. He later returned with a huge platter filled with peppery jumbo crab legs and two tiny silver utensils to open the crab legs.

After dinner, Tracy and Evan went dancing before walking along the beach. The sound of waves splashing against the huge rocks mingled with laughter and the salty aroma of the ocean were like paradise to Tracy.

She stopped and slipped her arms around Evan's waist, preventing him from moving. Tracy raised up on the tips of her toes and kissed him. "Thanks for a wonderful evening."

He returned her kiss. "Tracy, when I invited you, I intended for you to stay with me," Evan said.

"I have a room at the hotel."

"Are you sure you don't want to spend the weekend with me?"

"I think I'll keep my room," Tracy said. Not that his suggestion wasn't tempting, but she felt better staying at the hotel.

"Stay with me tonight," Evan said to her once they were inside his boat and heading to her hotel.

Tracy seriously considered Evan's invitation before making her final decision. She was aware of the circumstances, but she wanted to stay with him. "I think I'll stay in my hotel room while I'm here."

"Are you sure?" Evan drove the boat to her hotel.

"I'm sure," she said to him as he slowed and stopped at the hotel pier. "Tomorrow night, I'm taking you out," she promised as they got out and walked inside the building to wait for the elevator.

"I would like that." Evan gave Tracy a squeeze and grinned.

"I want you to dress very casual," Tracy said, thinking of a place on the beach she'd spotted while she and Evan were going to dinner. One couple was dressed in swimsuits. A blanket was spread on the sand, and there was a picnic basket on the table. She intended to check out the area the following day and find out how to go about entertaining on what appeared to be a private area of the beach.

"I'm looking forward to it." Evan chuckled as they took the elevator to her room and walked to Tracy's door.

Tracy kissed his jaw. "You'll need your swimwear."

He drew her to him then, smothering her lips with a hungry kiss. The captivating kiss made her wish that she'd accepted his invitation to spend the night.

"Good night, Evan," Tracy said before stepping out of his embrace and going inside her room. Afterward, she leaned against the door, savoring the evening she'd spent with Evan and his warm affection.

Twenty-one

The next morning after a breakfast of juicy orange slices and crimson strawberries covered with light cream, Tracy was about to spend her day shopping when she answered her door and saw Evan.

"Good morning," she greeted him, accepting his kiss.

"Hi," Evan spoke to her. "Are you ready to go?"

"I was going shopping," Tracy answered. If he had previously told her that he was coming for her this morning, she didn't hear him. "We didn't make plans to go out early today." She was going to check out the beach for the picnic she was planning for them later that night.

"We didn't, but I thought you might want to stay on my side of the island today. You can shop there."

Tracy agreed to go with him. She packed a bag with swimwear and a few other clothes just in case she didn't get back to the hotel in time to change for their evening out.

When they reached the boat, Evan said, "You're driving."

"Are you still sure you want me to drive your boat?" Tracy asked him.

"I'm sure you can handle it." Evan slid into the passenger's seat. "If you can drive that fast little car you own, you can drive this boat," he said, taking his sunglasses off the dashboard and putting them on.

"This is a high-powered boat, Evan."

"There's not much difference between this boat and your car."

"I'd rather drive it another time."

Evan chuckled. "Chicken."

"Oh no, you didn't say that!" Tracy got behind the wheel and put on her sunglasses, challenging Evan.

Evan's laughter floated out to her. He pointed to the key. "Start the engine, and drive slow."

"Uh-uh. This is a speed boat, right? You do not want me to drive slow." She gunned the motor.

"Tracy."

"Now who's the chicken?" she teased him. It wasn't long before they were on the opposite side of the island.

Tracy gathered her overnight bag and straw purse, remembering that after she checked out the beach area, she was going shopping for a picnic basket, a blanket, and dishes.

"I'll take that." Evan reached out and took her bag before they headed to his apartment.

"I have to work today, Tracy, but I promise you I'll be finished before nightfall." He led her to the guest bedroom.

As she observed the bedroom Tracy relished

Evan's good taste. A white canopy bed without the top was covered with a white satin spread. Two expensive paintings hung on the wall, and an oversized wicker basket was set next to the balcony door, filled with rich green ivy.

Tracy set her purse on the nightstand. "I love this room," she said to him while he set her bag inside the half-empty closet below sheets that were neatly folded on the top shelf.

"Thanks." Evan closed the closet door. "Be careful," he warned her again. Then he detailed the dangers on the water for what seemed to Tracy like the millionth time since she'd been on the island.

"I'll be fine, Evan. You worry too much."

"And with good reason," he said, folding her into his arms and grazing her lips with his.

"I'll see you tonight," Tracy said, pushing him toward the door. "Don't work too hard."

"I can't promise you that I won't work hard, but I will see you later."

Tracy watched him leave before she took a cap from her bag and pulled her damp hair into a ponytail. With that done, she searched for a phone book and found a catering company that would fill an order for her on short notice. If she was unsuccessful in securing reservations for the private picnic site she'd seen, she and Evan could always eat at home.

She put on the cap, grabbed her purse, and headed out, picking up the boat keys as she left the bedroom.

Just as she was leaving the building, Regina walked inside.

"When Grant told me that you were on the island, I had to come over and see for myself," she said in a warm, cheerful voice.

"I decided not to miss the opportunity."

"Good, now let's go shopping," Regina remarked, flipping Grant's boat keys. "I got the boat."

"Let's not waste time." Tracy was smiling now. Regina loved to drive anything, and she was pleased to be riding with Regina, instead of taking Evan's boat.

"Tracy, there's this shop on the other side of the beach, and sister, the clothes are beautiful."

Tracy joined Regina's laughter and good cheer as they sped across the water to the dress shops. It was hard to stay mad at Regina.

Tracy's ponytail bounced with the wind and water sprayed from underneath the boat, sprinkling Tracy's skin as Regina glided them across the ocean. They soon docked at the pier, along with other classic speed boats.

"Regina, when we're finished shopping, I would like for you to stop at a picnic site. I want to see if I need reservations."

"Yes," Regina said, and Tracy was surprised that Regina didn't inquire as to why she wanted to stop at that particular section of the beach.

Tracy got out, and their shopping spree began. After some time passed, they stopped to have lunch at a sidewalk café. She and Regina ate fruit salads and drank spring water.

"Tracy, you can tell me what was going on with you and Evan," Regina pried.

"If you must know," Tracy said between bites

of salad, "I called Evan's apartment one evening. . . ." She continued to tell Regina all the details.

"But listen." Regina laid her fork down and sat back in her chair. "When Grant and I got home last night, some little Miss Thing had the nerve to be standing outside his door, talking about how she wanted to speak to . . . my man in private."

Tracy stopped eating and chuckled. "I know I shouldn't ask, but what did you do?"

"Tracy, I asked her to do me a favor." Regina smiled impishly. "I walked her to the elevator and pushed the button."

Tracy continued to smile. "And?"

"When the door opened, I told her to go inside and push the button for floor one, so she could find the lobby."

Tracy smothered her smile and looked out into the crowd. "And Grant?"

"We went inside and had a good old time."

Tracy laughed. "Regina, you're too much. I don't know what I would've done."

"You probably would've flown back to Atlanta." Regina took a sip of water. "That woman was *not* spoiling my weekend."

After their shopping spree, Tracy and Regina headed back to Evan and Grant's apartments respectively, promising to see each other the next day.

That evening, Tracy showered and dressed before Evan got home. She pulled on a pair of baggy white pants over a two-piece thong bathing suit. By the time she finished dressing, the caterer was at the door, delivering the picnic basket that she had ordered.

Tracy checked the food before the young woman left, making sure the potato salad, crayfish tails, lobster, strawberries, coconut rum, and water crackers were all in order.

She tipped the woman, and then Evan walked in.

"Are we going on a picnic?" he asked, wrapping Tracy in his arms and kissing her.

"Uh-huh." Tracy answered, returning his kiss before ushering him to the bedroom to dress for their date.

The section of the beach that Tracy chose for her and Evan was quiet. Huge green palm leaves swayed gently in the wind. While ocean waves rolled and lapped onto the beach, Tracy set the picnic table with the china and silverware she had purchased earlier. She passed the rum to Evan to fill their glasses. Tracy spread a blanket on the area she'd chosen for them to relax on after their dinner and walk.

As the sun sank into the horizon, they ate and drank rum while sharing the events of the day.

After dinner was over, Tracy and Evan walked along the beach, stopping to smother each other's lips with light, whimsical kisses.

As dusk turned to night and stars resembling

diamonds sprinkled the royal-blue sky, they returned to their special place on the beach.

Tracy didn't resist when Evan pulled the tie on her baggy pants, making them drop to her ankles. She stepped out of them and unsnapped his pants. While he removed his pants she settled down on the blanket, and waited for him to join her. When he did, she snuggled against his rock-hard chest, nuzzling his lips until she heard strangled groans slip from them.

His lips found hers, sparking sensation and fervid passion to its peak. She savored each touch, like warm iron stroking her. Her blood seemed to race in slow motion, heating to a boiling point from his caress.

The next day, Frank stood on the pier, not far from Evan's boat. He noticed Tracy and another woman getting into the boat. Frank wasn't sure what was going on, but at that moment, he had a plan.

She has probably sold my diamond, Frank thought as he reached into his pocket and took out the phone he borrowed from his uncle. He punched in a number and waited for an answer. Evan and Tracy didn't know who they were dealing with. *Especially Evan,* Frank mused as he waited for the party on the other end to answer his call. He would demonstrate to them just how serious he was. "Hello?" He spoke to the person who answered the phone, and requested his desire for revenge. "And don't botch the job." Frank slipped the phone back into his pocket.

He planned to show Evan Maxwell who was more powerful, and he intended to do it today. Frank climbed into his boat, started the engine, and headed to his uncle's home on the other side of the water.

Twenty-two

Tracy and Regina headed out across the water to shop at a small boutique they'd noticed the day of their first shopping trip.

Tracy got out of the boat, almost colliding with a young man.

"I'm having trouble with my boat. Can I use your phone?" The man appeared to be in his early twenties. He was average height, brown skin, and wore tan work pants, a tan shirt and brown shoes.

"The pay phone is over there," Tracy said. Then she noticed another young man rushing toward Regina.

"I would rather use yours," he said, reaching for Tracy's purse.

"Give me my purse," Tracy screamed, reaching out to grab her purse from the man who had asked to use her telephone.

"No." He grabbed Tracy's arm.

Apprehension mingled with anger inched through Tracy's body.

"Give him the money, Tracy, so they can let us go!" Regina screamed.

"Shut up. We don't want money," one of the

men said to Regina. "You're not supposed to be here anyway. We're taking you with us because you just might call the police while we're taking her for a ride." He snatched Tracy closer to him.

"Please . . . let us go." Tracy pleaded with the man, struggling to free herself from his iron grip.

"No," he said, pushing her down to the boat. "Look ladies, we have a job to do. Nobody is going to get hurt."

"Unless it's necessary." Regina's captor patted the square-shaped bundle in his pocket. "So be quiet," he said to Regina. "When we drop her off, we will bring you back to the pier. Unless you want to party with us tonight."

Tracy's fear didn't allow her to hear a response coming from Regina. All she could think about was how afraid she was for her and Regina's life. She didn't know where they planned to take her, yet the men promised to return Regina safely to the pier. Dark fear hovered inside her and she thought she was going to be sick. If Regina was hurt, Tracy would never forgive herself.

"Help!" Tracy screamed, hoping a group of people she saw standing farther down the pier would hear her desperate cry and call the authorities, or at least try to help them.

"Shut up. We're going for a ride," the man whispered to Tracy.

Struggling to free herself, Tracy wished she'd paid attention to the men before she and Regina had stopped at the pier. But they had appeared harmless standing near a boat; Tracy hadn't given them a second thought.

"We can do this the easy way, or I can make this a horrible trip. You choose," the captor said to Tracy.

She settled down, fighting her tears and telling herself that she would be fine. Surrounded by danger, Tracy sat rigidly in Evan's boat as the driver sped out into the ocean. The salty scent from the ocean and the rollicking aquamarine waves seemed to have lost their mystique.

"Where are you taking us?" Tracy managed to ask over the clamor of the boat.

"You'll find out when you get there." He leaned close to Tracy's ear and spoke to her evenly. "Now, shut up."

His breath smelled like stale beer, making Tracy feel nauseated.

As they traveled further down the island, Tracy tried to control her fears and the dark imagination whirling through her. The crazy thoughts of what the men might do to her and Regina skidded across her mind, and with forced determination, she remained calm.

Through the boat's windshield and her impending tears Tracy could see that they were nearing the edge of the water and were heading toward the beach. From the distance, she noticed tall palm trees lining dry land. Long, green leaves rocked gently in the tropical wind.

The young man stopped the boat at the edge of the water, then slowly cruised up to the sand.

"Relax." He looked back at Tracy and motioned to his partner, who got out and pulled Tracy after him.

Tracy noticed Regina scurrying around, straining to see. Her face was wet with tears. "Tracy!"

"Be quiet." Tracy heard the driver say to Regina.

Tracy reluctantly allowed the man to pull her across the beach and toward a huge white house behind the palms. "Why are you taking me here?" Tracy managed to ask, trying hard to control the tremble in her voice.

"Lady, I don't ask questions, I follow orders, and we were ordered to bring you here."

None of this made sense to Tracy. She wanted to run, but even if she found the strength to tear away from the man, where would she run? She didn't know where she was. Would Evan find her, and would Regina remember the men's faces? What if the men never returned Regina to the other side of the island?

Minutes later, she stood at the front door beside the young man. He raised his fist and hammered against the wide white door. "Open the door," he yelled, moving over and peeking through the window of the house.

She heard a noise from behind the door. "Who lives here?" she asked the man who was still holding her wrist.

"You'll find out soon enough," he said. "Stop asking questions."

The door opened, and Tracy felt faint. She swayed against the young man as her vision began to blur. *Calm yourself,* she thought, not knowing whether or not she should pretend to be happy to see Frank Johnson. Her thoughts wavered back to Evan's warning. Sometimes, boats were hijacked and people were kidnapped—or worse.

"Hi," she said to Frank.

"Well, if it's not the lovely Miss Tracy." Frank grinned. "Come in." He motioned for the young man to release her. Frank grabbed Tracy, pulling her inside.

"I'll take care of you guys later. Thanks for the delivery."

Delivery? Tracy mused, scanning a room that led to a sunken living room. The shiny floors might have been beautiful to her if she weren't afraid. Instead, the room was like a prison. She might never be free to go home.

Frank closed the door behind them and released her hand. "Now, Miss Tracy, you're here to tell me exactly what happened to my diamond necklace."

Tracy was speechless. She felt as if her heart pounced into her throat. *Calm yourself!* she thought, moving away from Frank.

"I gave the necklace to Evan." Her voice was firm, and she even sounded brave to herself.

"I have not heard from Evan." Frank stared at her. "So, I took a trip to Atlanta, and I searched your house."

"You broke into my house?" Tracy asked as her fears flowed rapidly.

"Of course I did. You didn't give me a key."

"How did you get my address?"

"I have my own special way," Frank assured her.

Tracy didn't know what to think now. She knew one thing: she would free herself. She just hadn't figured out the details. "How well do you know Evan?" Tracy found it impossible to control the tremble in her voice.

"I know him well." Frank grinned, and Tracy saw his chalk-white teeth. "I don't know why you're afraid of me. Evan is no better than I am. Matter-of-fact, he's worse."

"What do you mean?" Tracy asked, her fear building even more. She didn't believe him, simply because she had never met anyone as awful as Frank Johnson.

"The only reason Evan looks good to you is because he missed out on fifteen years of prison, and I didn't."

"Fifteen years?" Tracy wanted to cry.

"Of course he did. He's a pirate, the same as I am. We take what we want, woman."

Tracy didn't want to believe him. But Evan knew a lot about the ocean, and he had warned her.

"I don't believe you."

"It doesn't matter whether you believe me or not. But if you want to know the truth, ask Evan why he wears an eye patch."

Tracy's fears swelled even more. She'd asked him, and he'd promised to tell her later. Frank must have sensed her fear, because his raucous laughter inflated the room.

"I can't trust him to do anything I ask him to do."

"I don't have the necklace," Tracy said, wanting to plead for her freedom. She had to get off the island. She had to get away from Frank and Evan. She prayed that the men who had captured her and Regina had the sense to return Regina safely. If her prayers were answered, Regina would notify the authorities that she'd been kidnapped.

"I'm not so sure who has my necklace. But somebody knows, and you or Evan are going to give it back to me."

At that instant, Tracy wished she'd continued her karate practice. But when Drake died, she'd given up the lessons and, in her fear, she didn't remember much, only to stay calm. *Gain strength and stay focused,* she told herself. Tracy wasn't sure how staying calm was going to help her now. She was too afraid to think straight. "I didn't know you and Evan were friends," Tracy said, looking around the room for an escape route and stalling for time.

"Ah, yeah. Evan and I were once the best of friends." Frank frowned, his light skin seemed to darken, as if some bad memory shadowed his mind.

Tracy realized that Evan was different from Keith, but now she was beginning to believe that he was as dangerous as the man that she was facing. She had to save herself.

Frank reached out for her, and she stepped back. "Don't touch me," she heard herself speak in a strange voice that didn't sound as if it belonged to her. She glanced around the room again, planning to use anything she got her hands on as a weapon.

"Where is Tracy, Regina?" Evan felt his blood rush to his face. If anything happened to her, he didn't know what he was going to do. He should've gone with Tracy to the boutique, but he and Grant wanted to play a game of dominoes with the men in their club.

"Two guys took her," Regina said, wiping tears off her face.

"Describe the men," Evan said. When the description of the men did not fit Frank, Evan wasn't sure if Frank had anything to do with Tracy's kidnapping. But he wasn't taking any chances. He knew Frank wanted the necklace, and he would do anything to get it.

"They took your boat." Evan heard Regina, but he could care less what happened to his boat. He could buy another boat, but he couldn't replace Tracy.

"Give me your keys," Evan said to Grant.

"I'm going with you," Grant said.

"I'm going alone." Evan caught the keys Grant threw to him. "Stay with Regina." He left the room and went to his safe, where he'd hidden the necklace. He had to take a chance, and he prayed that Tracy was with Frank. And if she were, he prayed that Frank wasn't crazy enough to harm her.

"If I'm not back in an hour, call the police," Evan said to Grant.

Grant nodded and consoled Regina, who was almost hysterical.

Evan ran from his apartment and down to Grant's boat. God, let Tracy be all right, he prayed as he raced in the direction of Frank's shack on the other side of the island. Tears burned his eyes, while visions of Frank attacking Tracy flicked across his mind. He slowed when he passed the coast guard. The officers had stopped a boat and were searching it. Evan realized that boat didn't belong to him. He pressed the accelerator, still praying and not stopping until he reached Frank's shack.

The small house was dark. He got out and ran to the shack. He didn't bother to knock. He hit the door with his fist, and it flew open. The house was damp and looked as if it hadn't been cleaned in several months. To make matters worse, there were no signs of Tracy or Frank. He didn't know what to do. *God, let me find her, and please God let her be safe*, Evan prayed as he ran back to his boat. He was unsure where to search for her before calling the authorities himself. He didn't know if he could wait for Grant to call them.

"He moved." Evan heard a woman's voice, and he turned toward her. She appeared to be in her sixties and was carrying a basket filled with green and yellow vegetables.

"Do you know the guy that lives here?" Evan asked the woman.

"Do I know him? Me and his mama were friends for years until she died."

Evan was not in the mood for a long conversation, nor was he interested in Frank's family history. "Where did he move to?"

"He moved in with his uncle." She pointed down the beach. "The first house behind the trees."

"Thanks," Evan said and got into his boat.

"I think a nice glass of wine will calm your nerves," Frank said to Tracy while he filled two glasses and handed one to her.

Without warning, Tracy struck his chin with her fist, forcing the glasses to slip from his hands. Red wine spilled from the glasses as they crashed to the floor.

Frank leaned back. "I have myself a fighter." He grabbed for her again.

Tracy ran past a table, picking up a silver candleholder. She pitched it in his direction. Frank ducked and went after her. Tracy threw a vase, striking Frank's chest. The expensive container fell to the floor, shattering into a million tiny pieces.

"Stop throwing things at me!" Frank yelled at her.

Disobeying his command, Tracy moved to a bookshelf that held more knickknacks than books. She hurled one small statue after another, but she missed her target, which was Frank's head. The objects struck Frank's arms and chest as he dodged. When the shelf was practically empty, Tracy noticed a sword hanging near the bookshelf.

"Don't you touch that sword," Frank said, ready to chase her.

Tracy yanked the weapon from the rack and began swinging, sending her kidnapper leaping and sliding on the spilled wine and to the front door.

Tracy watched him open the door and stumble over a large iron container at the edge of the small porch.

She watched as he winced in pain, holding his arm, and she wondered if his arm was broken. She stood over him, daring him to move.

"You're crazy!" Frank said, his face distorted.

"Shut up, or I'll hit you."

"Please! Put that thing down."

Tracy heard the roar of a boat, and she instantly prepared to protect herself from whoever was coming to Frank's house. She recognized Evan running toward her. Tracy turned toward him, lifting the sword higher.

"Tracy."

She heard Evan call her name. But she couldn't trust him now. According to Frank, Evan may or may not have changed. However, she had to trust him to get her to the other side of the island. Then she never wanted to see him again.

"Get away from me."

"Tracy, put the sword down."

She couldn't control her tears now. They fell freely, as she looked at the man she had loved and given herself to without question. She had trusted him, and he had endangered her life.

"I'm taking you home," Evan said, moving slowly toward her.

She laid the sword down.

"Are you all right?" Evan reached for her.

She stepped away from him. "Yes," she said through her tears. She wanted to go to Atlanta where she would be safer than she was on the island. She wanted to be alone with her fury, her fears, and her doubts. How had she made such a terrible mistake? Hadn't Drake warned her in her dream to run? Instead, she was in love with Evan, who was associated with kidnappers and thieves, and to top that off, she had returned to the island to be with him.

Evan realized that she didn't want any part of him. He reached into his pocket and took out the necklace. "This belongs to you," Evan dropped the necklace beside Frank.

With his good arm, Frank reached out and picked up the box. He flipped the top with his thumb. "Get that crazy woman out of here before she hurts me," Frank groaned.

"If you ever come after her again, Frank, *I'm* going to hurt you," Evan threatened.

"I wasn't going to hurt her," Frank said. "I just wanted my necklace."

Evan kneeled down on one knee beside Frank. "If you don't get my boat to me by tonight, you're going to wish that Tracy would've destroyed you with that sword."

"You'll have the boat tonight, Evan," Frank promised.

Evan rose from his kneeling position beside Frank, and Tracy walked toward Grant's boat, not wanting to hear the argument that was taking place between the men anymore.

"Tracy, I'm sorry," Evan said when he finally got in beside her.

She found a roll of paper towels on the boat's floor, ripped a sheet, and wiped her eyes. Instead of responding to Evan, she remained quiet as they headed back to his apartment.

"You're not going to hold what Frank did against me, are you?"

Only the bluster of the boat's motor and the whistle from a barge squelched the silence between her and Evan.

"Tracy, talk to me," she heard Evan say as he glided the boat to shore.

When they reached the dock, Tracy got out and started walking. She heard him call to her and heard his footsteps pound the pavement as she hurried to the nearest cab. She was through with Evan.

Evan finally gave up when Tracy got in the cab. He assumed that she was going to her hotel. He also assumed that their relationship was over. He took out his cellular and called Grant. It was only fair to let him and Regina know that Tracy was fine. He could hear Regina in the background asking Grant to let her speak to Evan.

"If anything happened to my girlfriend, I'm going to nail your hide to a wall and torture you myself," Regina cried.

Before Evan could defend himself, Grant was

talking to him again, asking if he needed any help.

"No, I'm fine," Evan said. "I'll see you soon." He shut the phone off and headed over to Tracy's hotel. He knew she was angry and hurt, but he had to make her understand that he had no control over Frank's actions.

When he reached the hotel, he hurried up to her room and knocked. He didn't get an answer. He took out his cellular, hoping that she would answer her phone.

"Hello?" He heard her tearful voice and his heart felt as if it would break.

Evan let out a sigh of relief. "Baby. . . ." Then she hung up, concluding any hope he had of speaking to her.

He knew it would be a week or two before he could speak to her now. He had business in England to attend to before he could return to Atlanta. He had finally planned to make his home in the States, because he wanted to be near Tracy as well as his new business. Now that Keith had sold his condo to Evan, he had no other choice but to move, although he wasn't sure how long he would live in the city if Tracy didn't want him.

Evan returned home and went to bed. That night, he didn't sleep.

Twenty-three

Tracy sat at the desk in her small condo study and wrote a check for the cleaning lady while the woman was upstairs in her bedroom closet, hanging her clothes. She had finally moved into her new apartment and had warned Hannah, Regina, Shun, and Betty not to give her new address to Evan.

Her summer had been filled with passion, romance, love, and danger. The summer was coming to an end, but her love for Evan was still fresh in her heart. I will forget him, she promised herself. It would someday seem like a dream that had turned into a nightmare. And when she took another vacation to get away from the stress and strain of her daily life, she would be careful not to shop at yard sales and would stay clear of strange men.

"I'm finished with everything," the cleaning woman said.

Tracy looked up from the check she'd just signed, handed it to the woman, and thanked her. "Good night," Tracy said, getting up from her desk and going to lock the door behind the maid.

At last she was alone, surrounded by beautiful new furniture and living in a lovely condo with new neighbors. And she was sadder than she'd been in a long time.

She went to work the next day, avoiding Keith as usual. Looking at Keith reminded her of her mistakes and the lover she'd chosen to rid from her life.

"Tracy, aren't you coming to the meeting?" Regina said.

"No," Tracy said, checking the information that she'd received from the title company on a property she was planning to close on.

"You know Keith is not going to like it if you're not there."

"You can tell him that I have two listings and one closing. The closing is taking place next week," she said, not looking at her girlfriend.

"Tracy, you need to talk to Evan. He's so upset."

"And?"

"According to Grant, it's been a long time since Evan has not been friends with Frank."

"Regina, will you stop trying to plead Evan's case?"

"I don't know Evan well, but I don't think he would associate with Frank."

"Okay, I'll go," Tracy said, getting up from her desk. She decided it was better to attend the meeting than to argue with Keith later.

During the meeting, Tracy kept her gaze lowered. Keith talked about the plans he had for

Maxwell Realty and the bonuses that he would dole out to the hardworking agents. There was an upcoming conference scheduled, and he expected everyone to attend. Tracy looked down at her pad, listening quietly, when Regina touched her with her elbow. Tracy glanced up, and her eyes swept over Evan. He stood near the door, looking as handsome as the first time she'd seen him.

Tracy lowered her gaze and continued to listen to the other agents report the number of listings or sales and closings they had accomplished.

Then Tracy announced her listings, closings, and sales. After she had finished, she excused herself and headed down the back stairs and out of the building. She didn't want to make close contact with Evan. She decided to start working from home until she was confident that Evan had given up on their relationship.

After the meeting, Evan spoke to Keith about his mother's new business in St. Hope Isle. He could've waited and talked to Keith later, but his desire to see Tracy was too strong. When he finished taking care of more business, he stopped at the mall and then drove to Tracy's house when he suspected she would be home. He'd watched her leave the meeting earlier and thought that maybe she had gone to an appointment.

Evan rang the doorbell and waited.

"Mr. Maxwell." A man who appeared to be

in his forties walked across the lawn, extending his hand to Evan. "How are you?"

"I'm okay," Evan said, wondering who this man was.

"I'm really interested in buying this house. Do you think you can show it to me tonight?"

It dawned on Evan that the man thought he was Keith, and the realization that Tracy had moved crept into his mind. "I'm Evan, Keith Maxwell's brother," Evan corrected him. "I didn't know that the person who lived here had moved."

"Yeah, I saw the ad and I thought . . . well, I'll call the agent." He turned and walked across the lawn.

Evan's hope for having Tracy in his life again dimmed even further. Maybe he and Tracy weren't meant to love each other after all. He gave up and went home.

Twenty-four

Tracy resumed her usual schedule, working at Hannah's when needed and volunteering at the WINOH center. The work consumed her, freeing her mind from her anguish and tormented heart. Evan was no longer a part of her life, and she was sure that she would eventually manage to cast all memories of him from her mind. Her heart would heal, and the summer they spent together would no longer hold a special place in her heart.

After Tracy arrived home, she dressed in black spandex pants and a short, matching top. She went to the small lounge next to Hannah's office and sank down on the seafoam-green sofa. The room was always peaceful and quiet, a place where Tracy could find solace. She and the other employees agreed that the room was a safe haven to unwind when they had a break.

Tonight she wasn't working at Hannah's, but she didn't want to stay home alone, struggling to keep her heart from aching from her loss. She stretched her long legs out on the sofa, propped a plump green pillow underneath her head, and took a magazine from the cocktail table. She began reading an article titled, "Widows Who Have Found True Love." The article reminded her of both the men who were lost to her. It seemed that getting Evan out of her system was harder than getting over the loss of Drake.

It would also have been much easier to forget Evan if Regina and Grant weren't so happy. Nonetheless, she was glad for her friend. Unlike Evan, Grant seemed to have been an upstanding, faithful, and honest man. Regina didn't talk much about him, but Tracy could see the sparkle in her eyes and hear the joy in her voice when his name was mentioned.

Tracy didn't hear the lounge door open, but she was aware of the soft thump when it closed. Without breaking her concentration, she continued to read the article. She assumed that Shun or another employee was also seeking refuge from the busy evening.

She turned the page, folding the magazine back and wishing that Shun wouldn't wear the same cologne that Evan wore. She'd smelled it on Shun twice since she had last seen Evan.

"Hi." Tracy looked in the direction of a familiar voice. Evan's tall, muscular frame towered near the door. He appeared more handsome than she remembered and was dressed in a dark suit.

The sound of his voice stirred warm, passionate feelings in her, feelings that she had fought to rid herself of. "Evan," she spoke, forcing herself to sound nonchalant. Still holding the magazine, she sat up.

Evan sat down beside her on the edge of the sofa. Leaning forward and resting his arms on his thighs, he locked his fingers together and faced her. Tracy watched him, taking in every inch of his features. His dark, wavy hair looked freshly trimmed. His eyes held a slight hint of hope, mingled with remorse.

"I was a mischievous kid. I hung out with Frank Johnson and his family." He looked at her, wanting to see her reaction.

So far, his explanation had no effect on Tracy. She'd heard portions of the story from Frank Johnson.

"I never robbed or hurt anyone," he continued, looking at her. "I was an angry young man, and I thought that if I disobeyed my father I could mentally hurt him. I was angry because he took me away from my mother."

Tracy listened, not taking her eyes off Evan as he made his confession and told her in detail how he was almost blinded in one eye once when he was out on the ocean with Frank and his uncles.

"I'm not the same person, Tracy. I grew up. I matured." He smiled down at her.

Evan's smile sent a new shiver of pleasure through her. But she continued to stay quiet. Evan felt the need to confess, to rectify the story he no doubt thought she had heard from Frank.

"After that night out with Frank and his uncles, my daddy took us . . . Keith and me to live with his sister in England."

Tracy dropped the magazine on the floor. "Why are you telling me all of this now?"

"Because I love you, Tracy."

"I love you, too, but I can't live my life thinking that I may be harmed because of something that happened to you years ago." Tracy astonished herself by expressing her most intimate feelings.

"I'm telling you all of this because I want you to trust me, Tracy." He looked away then, as if reliving the past. "On the island, many people still call me the 'Black Pirate.' "

"Are you still a pirate? Because if you are, I don't want to hear any more," she said.

"I'm not a pirate." He chuckled softly.

"Evan, I don't know what to think. You have—or had—dangerous friends," Tracy countered, wishing that she had gotten to know him better.

"Grant is the only friend I have." Evan covered her hand with his.

His touch was warm and soft but firm, and it sent ripples of pleasure through her, making her crave more of his sensual touch. But she couldn't. She'd promised herself that she would forget him and all the hope he brought to her life.

"Tracy, you're the first woman that I've ever wanted to marry."

"Are you proposing to me?" She sat up more then, her feet still on the sofa. How did he get inside the lounge, anyway? she asked herself.

"Will you marry me?"

"Evan, we're barely speaking. I don't think marrying you is going to solve our problem."

"*Your* problem," Evan said.

"Picture yourself in my position." Tracy eyed him carefully. "For the first time since my husband died, I fell in love. . . ." Her voice trailed off and she watched Evan. He seemed surprised. "I had fun, Evan, because I actually enjoyed spending time with you." She got up and circled the room slowly. She wanted him. But her apprehensions were strong. "And because I was your lover, I was kidnapped."

"I think I understand how you feel." He stood and walked over to stand in front of her, forcing her to stop pacing. "I have to go away." He reached into his pocket, pulled out a small jewelry box, and opened it.

Tracy caught her breath at the diamond engagement ring sparkling inside.

"I can't." She noticed the disappointment that seemed to settle in his eyes when she refused to take the ring.

"If you don't want to wear it, keep the ring, Tracy. If you're not interested in being my wife, I'll understand," Evan said, pressing the red-velvet box into her hand.

Tracy allowed him to fold her fingers over the box. "When are you coming back?"

"I don't know."

"Where are you going?" she asked. He was giving her a ring in hopes that she would agree to marry him, and she didn't know when she would see him again.

"I'm going to England."

"This isn't fair," Tracy lamented. But she was torn between her love for him and his past. "Why are you going to England?" she asked as jealousy reared its ugly head. *Doesn't the woman he once dated live there?* she asked herself.

"I have a few things I need to take care of."

"What do you have to take care of, Evan?" She gave him a knowing look. She saw an expression of shock cross his face, and she wished that she could have controlled her resentment toward the woman she didn't know but knew Evan had once loved.

He took her in his arms. "I'm going to take care of some business for my aunt. She's old and can't look after her business properly."

"I understand," Tracy said.

Evan leaned down and kissed her. His lips were hungry against hers, and without shame, she drank the sweetness from his lips. She knew that she should give the ring back and run to her car and go home. She was unable to fulfill the promise to herself, and now she knew she would never forget him, not as long as she had a ring to remind her. She untangled herself from his embrace. "I don't think this is a good idea," Tracy said, looking down at the ring box in her hand. "Take it." She pressed the tiny box into his palm.

Evan didn't pressure her. He set the box on the desk. "I want us to be together forever, Tracy."

"I think you should go," Tracy said. She was thinking with a clear mind now, but it was hard. Evan was like caffeine to her, she couldn't live with him and she couldn't live without him. She had to get him out of her system.

"So, we'll let nature take its course." He

reached inside his coat pocket and took out a card. "If you need me, or if you want to talk, I can be reached at this number." He walked out of the lounge and closed the door softly.

Tracy sank down on the sofa, considering Evan's proposal. She held the card along with the ring. She couldn't marry Evan.

Evan settled back in his plane seat and closed his eyes. He hadn't wanted to give Tracy an ultimatum, but he wanted her to love him as much as he loved her. He hoped that, by the time he returned, she would have made up her mind to be his wife. If she didn't, he was certain that he would be single for the rest of his life. Tracy was the woman for him. He knew it, and he wouldn't settle for anyone else.

Suddenly, Evan remembered that he hadn't asked Tracy for her new address. *It doesn't matter,* he decided. *I'll find her.*

Twenty-five

Weeks passed, and Tracy was still torn by her decision. Should she marry Evan? Except for her memories of him, Evan was out of her life. If she needed to talk to him, she could always call him. She sat at her desk and gazed at the card he'd given her the last time she'd seen him.

She crumbled the card and dropped it in the wastebasket beside her desk. Then she immediately retrieved it and pressed the crinkles out. She would be mailing the ring back to him. Her decision was final: She wouldn't marry Evan.

"Tracy, did you see this?" Regina came in, carrying the morning newspaper.

"No, what is it?" Tracy asked, reaching for the paper and reading the story.

> *Apartment owner Tracy Wilson is responsible for an affluent neighborhood being under siege with unclean and rowdy tenants. Neighbors plan to protest late tomorrow afternoon to force the owner to remove the tenant.*

Tracy felt her breath catch in her throat. The tenant she'd allowed the agent to rent her apartment to had sublet to several unauthorized people. According to the story, the police paid frequent visits to the property.

"Oh, my Lord," Tracy uttered, dialing the property manager's cellular number. When he answered her call, Tracy was livid. "How could you allow this to happen?" she asked. She had trusted him to maintain and pay close attention to the property that Drake and his family left to her.

"I'm already here, and I'm as shocked as you are. I didn't know others were living in this apartment."

"It's your job to know these things," Tracy shot back. "How bad is it?"

"It's bad," the property manager warned her.

"I'll be right over. In the meantime, make arrangements to have the female tenant evicted."

"I'll talk to you later, Regina," Tracy said, grabbing her purse and rushing out. She hated having the woman evicted, but she hadn't followed the rules. She was only supposed to have her child living with her. *What is she thinking?* Tracy wondered. She had reduced the rent for low-income, single parents who wanted to better their lives. The young woman had the opportunity to live among wonderful tenants in a quiet environment, but she chose to move other people in and disturb the neighbors.

Tracy raced through traffic, speeding to the apartment. She also had to stop the other tenants from protesting. Tracy pressed the brakes hard and slid into the apartment parking lot, bringing the car to a screeching halt.

The apartment was a disaster, to say the least. Food, dirty dishes, shoes, and clothes were scattered all over the kitchen and the living room floor. She didn't even want to think of the terrible condition the bathroom might be in.

"Mrs. Wilson, I see no reason for you to have me thrown out in the street with no place to go," the woman shouted. "I'm entitled to company and visitors."

"Fine. But your 'visitors' don't have to destroy the apartment or disturb the neighbors," Tracy reminded her."

"You're just like all those high-and-mighty witches in this town. You got nice stuff and don't want anyone else to have anything."

"Did you start the proceedings to remove her from this apartment?" Tracy asked the manager, ignoring the young woman's comment.

"Yes," he said.

"How am I supposed to enjoy myself if I can't have my man over when he wants to visit?" The young woman said to Tracy.

Tracy felt her face grow hot with anger. "What man?"

"My man," the woman said. "Y'all make me sick at that Women in Need of Help Center. All y'all do is sit up there pretending to help women like me. Nothing but a bunch of phonies."

"Don't talk to her," the manager suggested to Tracy.

Tracy took her purse and walked out, her temples throbbing from anger. She had tried to help the woman, thinking that she could work, save her money, and buy herself a home. But, instead the woman had vandalized her apartment and was ungrateful for any help offered. Tracy reached into her purse and took out her cellular. Regina answered her call on the first ring.

"Regina, meet me around five-thirty at that bar down by the office. Don't ask any questions. I'm having myself a strong drink."

"It's that bad?"

"The absolute worst," Tracy said, saying good-bye.

After she met Regina at the bar, Tracy was aggravated and exhausted. She took a hot bath and crawled into her bed. As she stared at the ceiling and the bands of light lining her walls from outside, she thought about Evan. *Lord, I love that man.* Without warning, she had found herself in love with him, and from that point on, that love grew. She sat up and took her purse from her nightstand, opened it, and took out the card that she had almost tossed in the garbage earlier that day. If she called him, he might think that she was considering his marriage proposal. She toyed with the idea of making the call as she traced her finger against the wrinkles she had tried to smooth out of the card. *Life is simply not fair.*

Tracy sneezed, suffering from a hay-fever attack. She got up and went to make tea from the leaves she'd purchased on the island. After the tea was ready, she poured herself a cup and went to her room, sipping the hot liquid as she climbed the stairs. By the time she reached her bedroom, her body was hot and craving Evan's touch. *"This tea is for your man,"* she remembered the woman saying the day she purchased the jewelry. Tracy sank down on the bed and slipped between the covers, realizing that the woman had sold her the wrong leaves. She yawned and was soon asleep, dreaming about Evan and the passion they'd shared.

Tracy still hadn't called him. Evan unpacked his bags in his new Atlanta apartment one Saturday afternoon. If he didn't have to meet with his manager, he wouldn't have returned to the city. Maybe Grant would want to take over the apartment. After all, he and Regina appeared to be doing well together. And taking over the apartment would save Grant hotel fare. He sat on the bed and allowed his thoughts to wander to Tracy and his love for her.

He understood her distrust for him. If it were not for Frank, he would have never known Tracy existed. But he had met her and loved her, and she was in his blood, his dreams, and when he was working, he thought about her. He had been waiting patiently at night, and sometimes during the day, for her call. Ultimately, Evan decided that some things weren't meant to be. He took off his pants and put on a pair of dark swim trunks. He draped a thick, white towel around his neck and walked out onto his balcony. The pool area was crowded. With a few laps in the water, he was sure to forget his troubles, even if only temporarily.

Twenty-six

One Saturday evening with nothing special to do, Tracy slipped into a black, low-cut bathing suit. She put on a matching beach shirt and walked down to the pool, scanning the area to see if Barry was among the crowd. He'd promised her that he was visiting friends that weekend and was bringing his swim trunks. Instead of seeing Barry, she noticed that all the yellow lounge chairs were occupied—except one.

It seemed that all her neighbors had the same idea. If their weeks had been as hectic as hers, surely they wanted to relieve stress and release tension in the late summer sun and cool water.

Tracy claimed the last chair and slipped out of her shirt before stepping into the pool and floating out into the deep end. She relished the water, allowing it to settle around her neck. Closing her eyes, she welcomed the peace, only to have it interrupted by laughter and loud splashes.

Tracy ignored the sounds. She was lost in her own world. She plunged beneath the water and swam to the other end. She reached out, gripped the edge, and pulled herself up, relaxing against the pool wall. Then she felt a pair of firm, strong hands resting on her waist. "Take your hands off me, Barry."

"Is that guy still trying to break us up?"

She swirled around and faced Evan. "Who are you visiting?" Tracy asked, astonished to see him. She peered over his shoulder, trying to see anyone behind him.

"I live here."

Tracy couldn't believe it. She remembered that Keith had owned an apartment in the building during his bachelor days. "You live in Keith's apartment?"

"I bought it." Evan said, lowering his head and brushing his lips lightly against hers.

With no further questions, Tracy revelled in his touch as he traced her lips with the tip of his tongue, parting them for a heated, drugging kiss. She slipped her arms around his neck and welcomed his passion. Evan's kiss was like a balm, healing and soothing her soul.

"I missed you," Evan said, smothering her lips with another kiss.

She missed him, too, more than she thought she could miss anyone. She stood on her toes and ravished his lips with a long, lingering kiss.

Tracy didn't hear the footsteps that stopped at the pool's edge. However, the voices were clear, cutting into her and Evan's pleasure.

"Shameful and disgusting," said a voice that sounded as if it came from an old, disgruntled woman.

She wanted to turn, but Evan held her close. "Don't look."

"Hannah should have let her daddy's sister raise that child," the woman said. "But she ruined her life. Got that jukejoint and kept that girl around all those men."

"And look who she ended up with," said another female voice. "Mavis and Baily Maxwell's boy."

Tracy felt Evan bury his face in her hair, chuckling softly.

"Evan, who are those women?"

"Someone that knows our relatives."

"Let's go inside," Tracy said, not wanting to listen to the women ridicule her and Evan any longer.

"She should be ashamed of herself. Her husband's not cold yet, and she's all hugged up with that good-for-nothing boy."

"That's the truth. Both of them need to be somewhere praying."

"I thought this was a singles condo," Tracy said to Evan before he leaned down and kissed her again. Most of the older single or widowed women Tracy knew, like Mrs. Peterson, lived in senior villages.

"Maybe they *are* single," he said after he kissed her.

"Let's get out of here." Tracy swam to the pool's ladder and climbed out of the water with Evan behind her. They dried off and sat on the lounge that Tracy had saved with her towel and jacket.

She began to pay attention to the women who were sitting at a table close to where she and Evan had been enjoying each other. Tracy recognized one of them. She was the woman who Hannah bought the herbs for her colds and flu from when Tracy was a girl.

Evan pulled Tracy up with him off the lounge. "I hope this means that we're together again and that you're going to marry me."

"What? You think I'm going to marry you without retesting the goods?" Tracy asked playfully, grabbing him around his waist. The moment she had seen him in the pool, she knew she would accept his marriage proposal.

"I was hoping you would say that, baby." Evan picked Tracy up and flung her over his shoulder.

"Put me down, you crazy man!" she screamed.

"No." Evan laughed. "My place or yours?"

"Mine."

They reached the elevator, and Evan set her down. Once outside Tracy's apartment, he took her key, opened the door, and lifted her over his shoulder again, carrying her to the bedroom.

Tracy couldn't control her laughter at Evan's primitive gesture. She bounced when he dropped her on the bed, and peals of laughter spilled from her, filling the room. "Oh, Evan," she said as he covered her body with his. "I do love you."

Evan looked at her, and from that point on, the real world slipped out of focus.

He unsnapped her top, and Tracy heard the damp material fall to the floor. He rose, pulling her bottoms away from her round hips. She watched as he took off his trunks.

Tracy rolled off the bed, and between kisses, she walked with him to the bathroom and turned on the shower. They stood under the spraying water, lathering each other and allowing the water to rinse their bodies. Evan's lips searched hers, and her touch wandered over his firm body. After the shower, Tracy backed out of the stall with Evan walking in front of her. She backed into the bathroom vanity, rested her hips against a thick, fluffy, gold towel, and pulled Evan to her. In their bliss, he explored her inch by inch. The only thing between them were the clouds of steam.

Tracy reached to the side, slid open the vanity drawer, and retrieved one foil packet. She ripped the edge to remove the protective shield and covered Evan's strong masculinity.

Evan inched into her with slow, measured strokes. Suddenly, the steamy room echoed with animalistic sounds mingling with soft, sultry murmurs.

Tracy and Evan clung to each other as they moved to the bedroom. Still half delirious, she felt him curve his palms around her waist and set her down on the king-sized bed.

After a short nap, they showered, dressed, and went for a ride. Tracy knew she was making the right decision to marry Evan.

"Evan Maxwell, you're a naughty man. How dare you run off and elope without telling your mother," Mavis said, then smiled. "Where is your wife?"

Evan pushed his chair away from the table and went to the back of Hannah's office to get Tracy. He stood in the office doorway for a few minutes, waiting for Hannah, Betty, and Regina to finish telling Tracy exactly what they thought of her.

"I'm glad she called and told me she was getting married last night." Hannah beamed. "Tracy, I'm happy for you."

"Thanks, Hannah," Tracy said.

"Well, I never thought I would see the day." Betty laughed. "Tracy, girl, you can keep a secret."

"Everybody, listen. I didn't mean to keep a secret. It was a spur-of-the-moment thing."

"Regina, you don't look surprised." Betty turned to her.

"Tracy told me."

"Little sneaks." Mavis stood at the door. "I thought I better come back here and meet my daughter-in-law before she and Evan run away again."

Evan chuckled. "It's not like that." He draped his arms around his mother's shoulders. "Everybody, this is my mom, Mrs. Mavis Maxwell," Evan said. In a low voice for only his mother to hear, he said, "I called you last night. When you didn't answer, I left a message."

Mavis smiled.

While the women introduced themselves to Mavis, Evan nodded his head, motioning for Tracy to join him. "Let's get out of here," he said. Everyone stood in the room, arguing about who knew that Tracy and Evan were even thinking about marriage.

Tracy and Evan seated themselves at a table that was large enough for the family and their farewell lunch. It wasn't long before Keith and his wife joined them.

"I guess you knew about the marriage, Keith?" Hannah asked Tracy's broker.

"Hannah, I was just as surprised as you all are," Keith announced.

"Come on guys, be good sports," Evan chuckled. "It's not that bad."

"No, it's worse," Mavis said.

"Okay. Tracy and I will have a real wedding as soon as we're back from our honeymoon." Evan looked at Tracy. "Right, baby?"

"Right," Tracy agreed.

"Whoever heard tell of a wedding after the honeymoon?" Betty asked.

By then, everyone was talking at once. The honeymoon issue turned into a debate. Most of the people in the party were sure that Evan and Tracy didn't need a honeymoon. Others argued that the entire idea of marriage was ridiculous. However, the whole conversation was in good humor.

"Evan, let's go," Tracy whispered to him, taking his hand in hers.

"People," Evan yelled over the noise, "if you'll excuse us, Tracy and I have a flight to catch."

Tracy hugged Regina. "You and Grant must have a wedding soon." She giggled.

"We will, Tracy." Regina smiled.

Tracy hugged Hannah. Their tears of joy mingled.

"Have fun," Hannah finally said.

"I intend to have the *best* time." Tracy released her sister and hugged Jordan and Shun.

Tracy and Evan said good-bye to their loved ones and took their flight to England.

They knew in their hearts and souls that their love would last forever. Through all their trials and ordeals, they had found in each other a true soul mate.

COMING IN APRIL 2001 FROM
ARABESQUE ROMANCES

__HIS 1-800 WIFE

by Shirley Hailstock   1-58314-157-X $5.99US/$7.99CAN

Fed up with her meddling family, Catherine Carson had a plan . . . make a deal with a nice guy who would agree to marry her for six months, then divorce. She knew Jarrod Greene was just the man for the job—until he sparked an unexpected desire. Now, Catherine must discover what she really wants if she's to find everything she's ever dreamed of.

__DANGEROUS PASSIONS

by Louré Bussey   1-58314-129-4 $5.99US/$7.99CAN

It's been eighteen years since Marita Summers found herself caught up in a powerful romance—and entangled in a shocking crime that nearly destroyed her life. Marita vowed never again to let her heart rule her head. But now, drawn to a family friend, she once again enters a shadowy world of sweeping passion . . . and peril.

__A ROYAL VOW

by Tamara Sneed   1-58314-143-X $5.99US/$7.99CAN

As heir to the throne of an island nation, Davis Beriyia's life has been planned out for him, including who he will marry. Determined to have one last chance at freedom before his marriage, he disguises himself as a building handyman. But when he falls for Abbie Barnes, Davis realizes that he would trade his kingdom for the chance to win her heart.

__DREAM WEDDING

by Alice Greenhowe Wootson

1-58314-149-9 $5.99US/$7.99CAN

If sparks aren't flying with her fiancé, Missy Harrison doesn't care—she had her fill of passion and turmoil in high school with Jimmy Scott. Or so she thought. On the way to her hometown to finalize the last-minute wedding details, her car breaks down, and Jimmy shows up in the tow truck . . . looking better than ever.

Call toll free **1-888-345-BOOK** to order by phone or use this coupon to order by mail. ALL BOOKS AVAILABLE APRIL 1, 2001.

Name_____

Address_____

City_____ State_____ Zip_____

Please send me the books that I have checked above.

I am enclosing $_____
Plus postage and handling* $_____
Sales tax (in NY, TN, and DC) $_____
Total amount enclosed $_____

*Add $2.50 for the first book and $.50 for each additional book.

Send check or money order (no cash or CODs) to: **Arabesque Romances, Dept. C.O., 850 Third Avenue 16th Floor, New York, NY 10022**

Prices and numbers subject to change without notice. Valid only in the U.S. All orders subject to availability. **NO ADVANCE ORDERS.**

Visit our website at **www.arabesquebooks.com.**

SIZZLING ROMANCE FROM
FELICIA MASON

USE COUPON ON NEXT PAGE TO ORDER THESE BOOKS